A FATHER'S RESOLVE

AN INVESTIGATION TO FIND DAUGHTER.

R.K.DARSHAAN

This Book is dedicated to those

who have lost their

CHILD...

And to my

Parents, teachers, and friends

who have

supported and encouraged me

Contents

Contents

Foreword

This is a story of love, sacrifice, and unyielding determination. At its core lies Loki, an ordinary man thrust into extraordinary circumstances when his daughter Lila is kidnapped. What begins as a desperate search for her spirals into a harrowing journey that tests the limits of his courage, loyalty, and humanity. Through Loki's eyes, we witness a father's lengths to protect his family, even when faced with impossible and unimaginable loss.

More than just a tale and suspense, this story delves into what it means to love fiercely and fight for what matters most. It is a reminder that even in the darkest moments, the bonds of family and the strength of the human spirit can light the way. Thank You for joining Loki on this journey - one that promises to stay with you long after the final page.

Preface

"Family is the anchor in the storm,
but what happens when the storm threatens to take it all
away?"

Acknowledgements

This story would not have been possible without the unwavering support and encouragement of those who inpire me daily. First and foremost, I am deeply grateful to my family, my teachers, and my friends for their endless love and understanding, especially during the late nights and countless hour spent bringing this tale to live.

To the readers who choose to embark on this journey: your time and imagination are invaluable, and I am humbled by your willingness to dive into this world. Lastly, a heartfelt thank you to everyone who believes in the power of storytelling - it is through stories we connect, heal, and find strength in the most unexpected places.

Prologue

The rain fell in steady sheets, drenching the narrow streets of Rivermist and masking the muffled cries of the man who stumbled through the dark. Loki's breath came in ragged gasps as he clutched his side, pain radiating from every fibre of his being. Blood trickled down his temple mingling with the cold raindrops that refused to let up. The storm was relentless, much like the torment that clung to him like a second skin.

He paused beneath the shadow of a crumbling archway, his heart pounding with desperation. Somewhere out there, his daughter, Lila, was waiting - perhaps crying, perhaps afraid, perhaps worse. The thought ignited a fire in him, despite his battered body and the odds stacked against him. He clenched his fists, his gaze lifting to the horizon as lightning illuminated the jagged spires of the city. Loki knew that every step forward could lead to salvation or ruin, but turning back was never an option. Not for her. Not for his family.

This was the beginning of the fight he never asked for, but one he could never walk away from

CHAPTER ONE

THE WEIGHT OF THE WORLD

The dawn broke over the small town of Rivermist, a sleepy place tucked away between rolling hills and thick, whispering woods. Loki woke to the muted hum of life stirring outside his window: the distant clang of a blacksmith's hammer, the soft neigh of horses, and the gentle rustling of leaves in the morning breeze. His alarm clock had long since stopped working, and he relied instead on the cries of the town crier who called the time from the square every morning.

Loki stretched, his limbs aching from yet another restless night on the thin mattress that served as his bed. His room was modest, to say the least—a single cot pushed against the wall, a chipped wooden desk cluttered with half-finished projects and scribbled notes, and a window that barely let in enough sunlight to make the room feel alive.

At twenty-nine, Loki had already become accustomed to the grind of life. His days began before sunrise and ended long after the town's lanterns were snuffed out for the night. He worked as a repairman, fixing everything from leaky pipes to broken carts, anything that would bring a few coins into his pocket. But the money was never enough.

Downstairs, the sound of laughter and clinking dishes broke through the quiet. Loki smiled faintly as he descended the creaking staircase into the kitchen, where his family was already gathered.

"Morning, Loki," said Freya, his younger sister, who was balancing a pot of porridge in one hand and a plate of bread in the other. At sixteen, Freya had a spark in her that Loki admired but sometimes worried about. She had inherited their mother's fiery spirit and sharp tongue, which often got her into trouble.

"Morning," Loki replied, rubbing the sleep from his eyes.

At the table sat his mother, Ingrid, her hair streaked with silver and tied back in a loose braid. Her hands were busy knitting a scarf, the rhythmic click of the needles adding a comforting cadence to the room. Despite the worry lines etched into her face, her eyes were warm as they met Loki's.

"You're up late," she teased gently.

"I'm always late," Loki shot back with a grin. "You just don't notice because you're always working."

His mother chuckled softly. "It takes work to keep this family running."

Across the table sat the youngest of the family, eight-year-old Erik, who was wolfing down his breakfast with the enthusiasm only a child could muster. Erik was the heartbeat of their home, a bright and curious boy who found wonder in even the smallest things. His laughter could light up the darkest days, and Loki often went to great lengths to keep it that way.

"Guess what, Loki!" Erik exclaimed, his mouth still full of porridge.

"What?" Loki asked, grabbing a piece of bread from the plate Freya had set down.

"I saw a deer outside this morning! It was huge, with big antlers and everything!" Erik threw his arms wide for emphasis, nearly knocking over his cup of milk.

"That's great, buddy," Loki said, tousling the boy's hair. "Maybe one day you'll catch one."

"I don't want to catch it," Erik said, frowning. "I just want to be its friend."

The room filled with laughter, a brief reprieve from the weight that seemed to linger just beneath the surface of their lives.

But as the morning wore on, the reality of their struggles crept back in. The pantry was nearly empty, and the few coins they had left would barely stretch to buy enough food for the week. Loki glanced at his mother, who had stopped knitting and was now staring out the window with a distant look in her eyes.

"I'll take on some extra jobs today," Loki said quietly as if reading her mind.

"You're already working yourself to the bone," Ingrid replied, her voice tinged with worry.

"It's what I have to do," Loki said firmly.

Freya, who had been listening in silence, finally spoke up. "I could start helping. Maybe I can work at the market or—"

"No," Loki interrupted, shaking his head. "You need to stay in school. That's not up for debate."

Freya's lips pressed into a thin line, but she didn't argue. She knew Loki was stubborn when it came to protecting the family, even if it meant sacrificing his own needs.

Later that morning, as Loki prepared to leave for work, Ingrid spoke up. "Loki, I forgot to tell you. We'll be leaving for Aelstone tomorrow morning."

"Aelstone?" Loki asked, turning to face her.

"Yes," Ingrid replied. "My cousin's farm. They need help with the harvest, and they've promised to pay us for our time. Freya and Erik will come along to help. It'll only be for a few weeks."

Loki's brow furrowed, concern flashing in his eyes. "You'll be gone for that long?"

"It'll be good for us," Ingrid said gently. "And it'll give you some space to focus on your work without worrying about us for a while."

Freya grinned. "Don't miss us too much, big brother."

"I'll try," Loki said with a small smile, though the thought of an empty house weighed heavily on his heart.

The rest of the day passed quickly, with everyone busy preparing for their trip. By nightfall, the bags were packed, and the house felt strangely quiet. Loki sat in the living room, watching Erik carefully place a small toy deer into his bag.

"Take care of them," Loki said softly to Ingrid.

"I always do," she replied with a reassuring smile.

The next morning, as the sun rose over Rivermist, Loki stood by the door and watched as his family piled into the carriage bound for Aelstone. Erik waved enthusiastically from the window, Freya rolled her eyes in mock embarrassment, and Ingrid smiled warmly.

"We'll be back before you know it," Ingrid said.

Loki nodded, his throat tight. "Safe travels."

As the carriage disappeared into the distance, Loki turned back to the empty house. The laughter and warmth were gone, leaving only silence behind. He took a deep breath, steeling himself for the days ahead. For now, the weight of the world rested squarely on his shoulders.

CHAPTER TWO

THE STORM WITHIN

The air between Loki and his daughter, Lila, had been strained for weeks. Conversations were brief, interactions cautious, and every glance exchanged felt like stepping onto fragile glass. The fight, when it finally happened, was like a dam breaking after too much pressure, and it left cracks that neither of them knew how to repair.

Lila was seventeen—fiercely independent, headstrong, and unrelentingly curious about the world beyond their small town. She carried herself with an energy that could either light up a room or scorch everything in her path, depending on the day. Loki saw so much of her mother in her, and perhaps that was why their arguments hurt so much.

It had started with a door left ajar.

Loki returned home late one evening after fixing the axle of a merchant's cart. The house was dark except for a faint glow coming from Lila's room. He glanced at the kitchen—plates from dinner sat unwashed in the sink, and a half-empty mug of tea was left on the counter. He sighed, weariness pressing on his shoulders as he climbed the stairs.

Her room was empty.

The window was open, curtains fluttering in the cool night breeze. Loki's heart sank as he noticed the stack of books on her desk, untouched, and the jacket she always wore, missing from its hook.

He waited in the living room, every tick of the clock echoing like thunder. By the time she crept back through the door just before midnight, Loki was sitting on the couch, his arms crossed and his jaw tight.

"Where were you?" His voice was calm, but the tension was unmistakable.

Lila froze in the doorway, her shoes caked with mud and her hair tousled by the wind. "Out," she said flatly, avoiding his gaze.

"Out where?" Loki pressed, rising to his feet.

"Does it matter?" she snapped, the sharpness in her voice cutting through the room.

"Yes, it matters!" Loki shot back. "You disappeared without a word, and it's the middle of the night, Lila. What were you thinking?"

Lila's eyes flared with anger. "I was thinking that I'm not a child, Dad! I don't need your permission to go for a walk!"

"A walk?" Loki's voice rose, the frustration he'd been holding back spilling over. "You expect me to believe you've been wandering around town for hours, in the dark, with no explanation?"

"Maybe if you trusted me, I wouldn't have to sneak out!"

The words hit like a hammer. Loki's fists clenched at his sides, his nails digging into his palms. "This isn't about trust, Lila. It's about safety. Do you have any idea what could happen to you out there?"

"Of course I do!" she shouted, stepping closer. "I know exactly what's out there because I'm not blind! But you treat me like I am. You're so busy trying to protect me from everything that you don't even see me!"

Her words pierced through him, leaving a silence that felt heavier than anything Loki had experienced in years.

Lila's breathing was ragged, her cheeks flushed with frustration. "I'm not Mom," she said softly, her voice trembling. "I'm not going to disappear like she did."

Loki staggered as if he'd been physically struck. The room felt smaller, suffocating. "Don't," he whispered, his voice hoarse. "Don't bring her into this."

"Why not?" Lila shot back, tears welling in her eyes. "It's what this is about, isn't it? You're so afraid of losing me the way you lost her that you're holding on too tight. But I'm not her, Dad. I need to live my own life!"

Her words echoed in the silence, each one cutting deeper than the last. Loki opened his mouth to respond but found he couldn't.

Without another word, Lila turned and stormed up the stairs. The slam of her bedroom door reverberated through the house like the final note of a dirge.

Loki stood there in the empty living room, the weight of her accusations settling over him like a heavy cloak. He wanted to chase after her, to say something—anything—that would make her understand. But instead, he sank onto the couch, burying his face in his hands.

As the clock ticked on and the house fell silent, Loki sat alone in the dark, wondering if he was losing the one person he'd fought so hard to protect.

CHAPTER THREE

SILENT BRIDGES

The morning light seeped through the cracks in the curtains, casting faint lines across the worn wooden floor of their modest home. Loki sat at the edge of the kitchen table, fingers drumming a nervous rhythm against the surface. His gaze flickered toward the staircase every few moments, ears straining for the sound of footsteps that never came.

Lila hadn't spoken to him since the argument. She had come down briefly the evening before to grab a glass of water, her movements quiet and deliberate, her eyes fixed on the ground. Loki had tried to meet her gaze, to offer a small smile, but she had turned away before he could muster the courage to say anything.

It wasn't anger that clung to her—it was something heavier, something Loki couldn't quite place.

Now, as the clock ticked steadily in the background, he wrestled with the weight of his guilt. He had spent years patching up broken fences, repairing rusted gears, and fixing everything around him. But when it came to Lila, he wasn't sure how to mend what had been fractured between them.

The sound of a door creaking upstairs jolted him from his thoughts. He stood up instinctively, his chair scraping against the floor, but stopped himself before taking a step. He didn't want to scare her off, didn't want her to think he was waiting to pounce on the first opportunity to talk. Instead, he busied himself with the kettle, pouring water over fresh tea leaves and pretending not to notice when she finally descended the stairs.

Lila moved quietly, her shoulders hunched and her hair falling over her face like a veil. She paused at the base of the staircase, glancing at him briefly before walking toward the door.

"Lila," Loki said softly, his voice barely louder than a whisper.

She didn't stop. She grabbed her jacket from the hook by the door and slipped outside, closing it gently behind her.

Loki stood there for a moment, the warmth of the tea forgotten in his hands. A part of him wanted to follow her, to make sure she was okay, but he knew that pushing her would only drive her further away. He set the mug down, grabbed his jacket, and decided to wait—near, but not too near.

Outside, the air was crisp and carried the scent of damp earth. Loki watched from the edge of the porch as Lila wandered into the field behind their house. Her pace was slow, her hands stuffed into her jacket pockets, her head bowed as if carrying an invisible weight.

He followed at a distance, his boots crunching softly against the frost-covered grass. Lila made her way to the lone oak tree that stood at the edge of the property, its gnarled branches reaching skyward like a silent sentinel. She sat at its base, knees drawn up to her chest, and stared out at the horizon.

Loki stayed back, leaning against the fence post a few dozen yards away. From here, he could see her but wouldn't intrude. He thought about calling out to her, offering some excuse to come closer—a question about lunch, maybe, or a comment about the weather. But every time he opened his mouth, the words caught in his throat.

She wasn't ready to talk.

Instead, he let his mind wander, searching for answers he didn't have. He thought about the little girl who used to run through these fields, her laughter ringing out like bells in the wind. He thought about how, even then, she had a way of retreating into herself when something was wrong. A scraped knee or a broken toy didn't lead to tears; it led to silence. She had always been like that—a storm brewing quietly under the surface, waiting for the right moment to break.

Hours passed, or maybe only minutes—it was hard to tell. Lila hadn't moved from her spot under the tree. Loki had fetched a blanket from the house and placed it gently on the fence post before returning to his vigil. He wasn't sure if she had noticed it, but that didn't matter. It was there if she needed it.

As the sun began its descent, painting the sky with hues of orange and pink, Lila finally stood. She brushed the dirt from her jeans and turned back toward the house, her steps slow and deliberate.

Loki straightened as she approached, his hands tucked into his pockets to hide the nervous fidgeting of his fingers. She walked past him without a word, her eyes focused straight ahead. But just as she reached the porch, she paused.

For a moment, Loki thought she might say something. She glanced over her shoulder, her expression unreadable, and their eyes met.

It was brief, fleeting, but at that moment, Loki saw a glimpse of something he hadn't seen in days. It wasn't forgiveness, not yet, but it was a crack in the wall she had built around herself.

Lila disappeared into the house, leaving the door ajar behind her.

Loki lingered by the fence for a while longer, watching as the stars began to prick the evening sky. He didn't know if she'd ever come to him on her own or if he'd have to keep trying, keep waiting, keep hoping.

But for now, that brief look, that tiny crack, was enough.

CHAPTER FOUR

It began as an ordinary day, one that promised nothing out of the ordinary. Loki woke up to the faint sound of birds chirping outside the window and the rhythmic creak of the old house settling under the morning sun. The air was cool, and the sky outside glowed with pale gold as the first light of dawn crept across the town.

Lila wasn't in her room when Loki passed by to knock on her door. At first, he thought little of it—maybe she had gone to the backyard or the field behind the house like she often did when she needed time alone. She hadn't spoken much since the argument, but Loki was starting to see glimmers of her coming back around.

He called out her name casually, a quiet, almost hesitant "Lila?" as he poked his head into the kitchen. Her plate from the previous night was still on the counter, untouched. Loki frowned.

She always ate something, even when she was upset.

The house was silent except for the ticking of the clock on the wall, and an uneasy feeling began to creep over him.

By mid-morning, Loki was walking the perimeter of their small property, hands in his pockets and a forced casualness in his step. He told himself he was simply looking for her, not panicking—Lila was sixteen, independent, and capable. She had probably gone to town to visit friends or clear her head.

But as he checked the oak tree where she often sat, the empty clearing brought a pang of discomfort. He scanned the horizon, his eyes darting to every familiar landmark, hoping for a glimpse of her figure in the distance. Nothing.

When he returned to the house, he noticed the absence of her jacket on the hook by the door. A small detail, but it made his heart sink. Wherever she'd gone, she had left deliberately.

"She'll be back," he muttered under his breath, trying to reassure himself as he stepped into the kitchen and brewed a fresh pot of tea.

But as the day wore on and the sun began to dip below the horizon, Loki's unease grew. By evening, he was pacing the length of the house, his mind conjuring a thousand possibilities, each one worse than the last.

The first night passed in restless silence.

Loki sat by the window, his hands gripping a mug of cold tea, staring out into the darkness. Every creak of the house and the rustle of the wind outside made him sit up straighter, his heart racing with the hope that it was her. But the hours stretched on, and the only sounds were the lonely cries of night birds and the occasional howl of a distant dog.

He barely slept, his mind a constant loop of worry.

Where could she have gone?

Was she safe?

Had something happened?

By dawn, he was running on nothing but nerves and coffee. He decided to head into town to see if anyone had seen her. The streets were already stirring with the bustle of morning, but no one had any answers. Shopkeepers shook their heads, and a couple of kids who knew Lila shrugged when Loki asked if they'd seen her.

"Sorry, Mr. Larsen. Haven't seen her since last week."

Loki's heart sank further.

By the second day, the dread had become unbearable.

He checked every place he could think of: the field, the town square, the small wooded area behind the church where Lila sometimes went to sketch in her notebook. Each space felt like a punch to the gut, the absence of her presence was more palpable with every passing hour.

Loki began asking himself questions he didn't want to answer. Had he driven her away? Was this her way of punishing him for being too protective, too controlling? Or was it something worse?

The thought of her being in danger, of something happening to her that he couldn't fix, made his chest tighten until it was hard to breathe.

By the second night, the house felt like a tomb. Every corner, every shadow seemed to whisper her name, mocking him with her absence. Her room remained untouched, her bed neatly made, the faint scent of her favourite lavender lotion still lingering in the air. Loki stood in the doorway, staring at the room as if she might suddenly appear, her familiar grin breaking through the tension.

But she didn't.

Loki didn't know how much more he could take. He hadn't eaten in two days, and the exhaustion was beginning to wear him down, but he couldn't stop. He kept pacing the house, the yard, the streets—anywhere he thought she might have gone.

He asked neighbours, people in town, even strangers passing through. Each time, he was met with the same answer: No one had seen her.

The second night was colder than the first. Loki sat by the window again, his eyes bloodshot and his hands trembling. He hadn't cried yet—not because he didn't feel like it, but because he couldn't afford to break down. Not yet.

The silence of the house was oppressive, a weight pressing down on him from all sides. He couldn't stop thinking about her—her laugh, her stubbornness, the way she used to curl up on the couch with a book, completely lost in her world.

Where was she now?

As the first light of dawn broke on the third day, Loki realized he couldn't keep this up. He needed to do something more—call someone, organize a search party, go to the police if he had to. But even as he thought about those steps, a deep, gnawing fear gripped him.

What if she was gone for good?

What if he had failed her, just like he had feared all along?

The thought made his knees buckle, and he sank to the floor, his head in his hands. He didn't know how to move forward, how to keep going without her.

All he could do was wait and hope—hope that Lila would walk through the door, that this nightmare would end, and that he hadn't lost her forever.

CHAPTER FIVE

Loki's world had shrunk to the bare essentials of survival: the endless pacing, the sleepless nights, and the gnawing ache of uncertainty. He'd spent the last three days torn between fury and despair, haunted by the echo of Lila's laughter in the empty house. He had replayed every moment of their last conversation in his mind, dissecting it for clues, wondering if there had been something he missed, some sign he hadn't seen.

But this morning was different. It wasn't just the quiet that unnerved him—it was the strange sense that something was coming, like the sharp drop in temperature before a storm.

The first sign was the envelope.

It arrived with the regular mail, tucked between a stack of bills and advertisements. Loki didn't notice it at first; his hands were trembling too much to sort through the pile properly. But as he sat down at the kitchen table, the plain white envelope slipped free and landed on the floor.

Loki froze. His breath hitched as he stared at it. There was no return address, just his name scrawled in uneven black ink across the front: Loki Larsen.

His hands felt clammy as he picked it up. The paper was cheap and rough against his fingertips, the kind you'd find in bulk at any corner store. He flipped it over and hesitated before tearing it open. A single sheet of paper fell out, folded neatly in half.

When he unfolded it, his heart stopped.

We have Lila. $50,000 by the end of the week, or you'll never see her again.

No signature, no instructions, nothing else. Just those few, chilling words written in the same uneven scrawl as his name on the envelope.

Loki's hands shook so violently that he had to set the paper down before he tore it. His mind raced, thoughts colliding in a chaotic spiral of fear and disbelief.

Kidnapped.

It felt impossible. Absurd. This sort of thing didn't happen to people like him, in places like this. But the words on the paper were real, staring back at him like a living thing, mocking his disbelief.

The hours that followed passed in a haze. Loki read the note over and over again, searching for any hidden meaning, any clue that might tell him who had sent it or where Lila was. But there was nothing. He inspected the envelope, the paper, even the ink, but all of it was maddeningly nondescript.

He thought about going to the police, but the note didn't leave him with much to work with. And then there was the unspoken fear that gnawed at him: What if they're watching me?

He tried to think rationally, but it was impossible. Every scenario his mind conjured was worse than the last. What if she was hurt? What if they'd already...

No. He couldn't go there.

Instead, he threw himself into action. He called everyone he could think of—neighbors, old friends, even distant acquaintances—asking if they'd seen or heard anything unusual in the last few days. He searched the house again, desperate for some clue he might have overlooked. But all of it led to the same, crushing dead end.

By nightfall, Loki was a wreck. He hadn't eaten since the morning, and his body ached from the tension he carried in every muscle. He sat at the kitchen table, the note spread out in front of him like a puzzle he couldn't solve.

He had $50,000 saved. Barely. It was everything he had scraped together over the years, money he'd intended to use for Lila's future. College, a better life, something brighter than the one they'd been given.

But if it meant getting her back, he'd give it up without hesitation.

He just didn't know how to start.

Around midnight, the phone rang.

Loki nearly jumped out of his chair, the shrill sound cutting through the oppressive silence like a knife. He grabbed the receiver, his hands trembling as he pressed it to his ear.

"Hello?"

There was a pause on the other end, long enough to make his heart race.

"Mr. Larsen."

The voice was male, low and distorted, like it had been altered to mask the speaker's identity. Loki's grip on the phone tightened.

"Who is this?" he demanded, his voice cracking with a mix of fear and anger.

The voice ignored his question. "Did you get my message?"

Loki's blood ran cold. His free hand gripped the edge of the table, knuckles white. "Where is she?" he asked, his voice shaking. "What have you done with my daughter?"

The voice chuckled, a hollow, mechanical sound. "You don't need to worry about her. She's alive, for now. But you'd better act quickly if you want it to stay that way."

Loki's heart pounded so loudly he could barely hear the words. "What do you want?"

"I already told you," the voice said, its tone flat and emotionless. "Fifty thousand dollars. Cash. No police, no tricks. I'll contact you again with instructions."

Before Loki could respond, the line went dead.

He stood there for a moment, the phone still pressed to his ear, the silence on the other end a deafening roar in his mind.

The note, the call, the voice—it was all real. And Lila was out there, somewhere, depending on him to save her.

But as he lowered the phone and stared at it, another thought crept into his mind. The voice. Something about it didn't feel right.

It wasn't just the distortion—it was the way the man had spoken, the choice of words, the pauses. It felt... deliberate. Calculated.

And for the first time, a seed of suspicion took root in Loki's mind.

Whoever this was, they knew him.

CHAPTER SIX

The night was merciless.

Loki sat on the couch in the dim living room, the single lamp casting long, jagged shadows across the walls. The letter and the memory of the voice on the phone replayed in his mind like a broken record. The words looped endlessly, their weight growing heavier with each repetition.

"Fifty thousand dollars. No police."

He leaned forward, elbows on his knees, and stared at his hands. They were shaking, though he wasn't sure if it was from fear or the exhaustion that had been building since Lila disappeared. His knuckles were raw, his nails bitten down to the quick.

The house around him felt like a stranger's home. The quiet wasn't comforting anymore—it was suffocating. Every creak of the old wooden floorboards and every groan of the wind outside made his heart race.

He looked toward the window. The curtains were drawn, but he felt exposed as if someone might be watching from the darkness beyond.

Were they out there? The people who had taken her? Were they laughing at him, waiting for him to crack?

Loki's mind began to wander. He thought of Lila—not as she had been during their fight, but as she was when she was little. He could see her, a bright, smiling four-year-old with wild curls and an insatiable curiosity. She used to follow him everywhere, her tiny hand clutching his finger as they walked to the park or the market.

"Papa, why's the sky blue?" she would ask, her head tilted up, her eyes wide with wonder.

And Loki would do his best to answer, even if he didn't always know.

Those were the good days. The days when he still believed he could give her the world, even if the world had never given him much.

But things had changed. As she grew older, the questions became harder to answer. Why don't we have as much as the other families? Why do you always work so late? Why can't I have the things my friends have?

He tried. God, he tried. But no matter how many hours he worked or how many sacrifices he made, it was never enough.

And now, he had failed her in the worst way imaginable.

The hours dragged on, each one feeling longer than the last. Loki didn't know what to do with himself. He couldn't sleep, couldn't eat. The thought of food made his stomach churn.

He tried to distract himself by cleaning the house, but it only made things worse. Everywhere he looked, there were reminders of her: the sketchpad left on the coffee table, the worn sneakers by the front door, and the small pile of clothes she had forgotten to take upstairs.

He picked up her jacket, the one she always wore, and pressed it to his face. It still smelled like her—lavender and something faintly citrusy. His chest tightened, and for a moment, he couldn't breathe.

"I'm sorry, Lila," he whispered, his voice breaking.

He didn't know if he was apologizing for the fight, for not being there when she needed him, or for not knowing how to fix this. Maybe all of it.

At some point, Loki found himself sitting at the kitchen table again, staring at the crumpled note.

Fifty thousand dollars.

It was everything he had, and yet it felt like nothing. He would have given them a million if it meant bringing her home, but money didn't solve everything. The note didn't guarantee her safety. For all he knew, they could take the cash and leave him with nothing.

The thought made him feel sick.

He tried to think rationally, to come up with a plan. But every idea seemed to crumble as soon as it formed. He wasn't a detective or a hero in a movie—he was just a father, scared out of his mind and completely out of his depth.

The minutes stretched into hours, and Loki was left with nothing but his thoughts.

What if he never saw her again?

The question clawed at him, sharp and unrelenting. It was the kind of thought he couldn't allow himself to entertain, but it was there, lurking in the shadows of his mind.

As the first light of dawn crept into the room, Loki realized he hadn't moved in hours. His body was stiff, his head pounding from the lack of sleep. He stood up, his legs unsteady, and walked to the sink.

He splashed cold water on his face, hoping it would wake him up, and give him some clarity. But all it did was remind him of how utterly drained he was.

He looked out the window above the sink, his eyes scanning the quiet street. The world outside looked so normal, so untouched by the chaos that had consumed his life.

How could everything be so ordinary when his world was falling apart?

Loki returned to the living room and sat down on the couch. He stared at the phone, willing it to ring, dreading the moment it would. He needed answers, but he wasn't sure he was ready for them.

The wait was unbearable, but it was all he could do.

For now, he was trapped in this limbo, caught between hope and despair, waiting for a call that could change everything.

CHAPTER SEVEN

The second day after the call was worse than the first.

Loki sat in his living room, surrounded by an oppressive silence that seemed to grow louder with every passing hour. The curtains were drawn, the television was off, and the ticking of the clock on the wall became an unbearable metronome counting down to something he couldn't predict.

He clutched his phone in his hand like a lifeline, his thumb hovering over the screen. He had already thought of calling the police a hundred times, but every time he moved to dial, the voice on the call echoed in his head:

"No police."

It wasn't a request; it was a threat. And the weight of it bore down on him like an anvil.

Still, doing nothing felt like a slow death. Every second that passed without action felt like a betrayal to Lila. But what could he do? The envelope, the note, even the call—all of it had been designed to leave him powerless, dangling on a string.

That morning, Loki forced himself to leave the house. He walked aimlessly through the neighbourhood, his hands shoved deep into his pockets, his head down. It was a cold, grey day, the kind that matched the weight in his chest.

The streets were quiet, with only a few cars passing and the occasional dog barking in the distance. He noticed things he hadn't before: the cracks in the pavement, the faded paint on the picket fences, the way the trees seemed to reach for the sky like skeletal hands.

It felt surreal like he was moving through a dream—or a nightmare.

As he turned a corner, he found himself standing in front of the park where he used to take Lila when she was little. The swings creaked in the wind, their rusty chains swaying gently. He could almost see her there, laughing as he pushed her higher and higher, her curly hair catching the sunlight.

The memory hit him like a punch to the gut. He leaned against the fence, struggling to catch his breath.

"Papa, push me higher! Higher!"

He squeezed his eyes shut, trying to block out the image. But it only made it worse. The memories came flooding back in vivid detail: her first steps, her first day of school, and the way she used to curl up on the couch with him to watch cartoons.

And now she was gone.

By the time he got back home, it was early afternoon. The house felt colder than before, emptier. He sat at the kitchen table, staring at his phone, willing it to ring.

It didn't.

Instead, he decided to revisit the envelope and the note. He had read it so many times by now that he could recite it from memory, but he spread it out on the table anyway. He studied every inch of the paper, every stroke of the uneven handwriting.

Something about it felt... off.

The handwriting wasn't messy in the way someone might write in a hurry; it was deliberate, almost careful in its unevenness as if the person had been trying to disguise their natural style.

It was a small detail, but it stuck with him.

He grabbed the envelope and inspected it again. The postmark was smudged, but he could make out part of the city name. It wasn't far from where he lived—just a few miles away.

Why would someone so close be doing this?

The rest of the day passed in a blur. Loki found himself pacing the house, checking and re-checking the locks on the doors and windows, as if that would somehow bring him closer to a solution.

He tried calling a few more people, though he didn't know what he expected to hear. Most hadn't seen Lila in months, and those who had didn't know anything useful. One of her friends mentioned that she had been acting "different" lately, but when Loki pressed for details, they couldn't elaborate.

It was maddening. Every conversation ended the same way: with him hanging up the phone, his stomach in knots, and his mind racing with questions that had no answers.

As night fell, the phone rang.

Loki snatched it up so quickly that he nearly dropped it. "Hello?" he said, his voice hoarse from lack of use.

There was a pause on the other end, long enough to make his heart pound. Then, finally:

"Did you get the money?"

It was the same distorted voice as before, cold and mechanical.

Loki swallowed hard. "I'm working on it," he said. "But I need proof that she's okay. I'm not giving you anything until I know she's safe."

The voice laughed—a hollow, unnatural sound that sent chills down his spine. "You don't get to make demands, Mr. Larsen. You'll do as you're told, or you'll never see her again."

"Please," Loki said, his voice cracking. "Just let me talk to her. Let me hear her voice."

The line went dead.

Loki slammed the phone down on the table, his hands shaking with a mix of rage and despair. He wanted to scream, to throw something, to do anything to release the pressure building inside him. But he couldn't.

Instead, he sank into the nearest chair, his head in his hands.

They weren't going to make this easy. Whoever they were, they knew how to play the game, how to keep him on edge, teetering between hope and hopelessness.

And yet, something about the call didn't sit right with him.

The way the voice had laughed—it wasn't just cruel; it was mocking. As if they knew something he didn't, something that would change everything if he found out.

Loki clenched his fists. He didn't know what that something was, but he was determined to find out.

That night, he couldn't sleep. The weight of everything pressed down on him like a physical force, pinning him to the bed.

He stared at the ceiling, his mind churning with questions.

Who were they? Why had they taken her? And what did they mean by that laugh?

For the first time since this nightmare began, a new thought crossed his mind—one that terrified him even more than the possibility of never seeing Lila again.

What if the person who had taken her wasn't a stranger?

CHAPTER EIGHT

The world outside felt alien as if every sound and shadow were conspiring against him. Loki wasn't a detective, a hero, or even the kind of man who thrived under pressure—but he was a father. That was enough.

He didn't wait for the next call. He wouldn't let himself sit in that suffocating silence for another second. If the kidnappers thought he'd wait idly by while they toyed with him, they were wrong.

Loki started by piecing together everything he had so far.

The envelope, postmarked from a nearby city, was the only physical evidence. He decided to start there. This time, he didn't go to the post office for answers—he went to the streets. He drove to the city, parking his old, beat-up car in a small alley off the main road.

The area was busy, the kind of place where people hurried past each other without so much as a glance. Street vendors called out to passersby, cars honked impatiently, and the hum of conversation filled the air. It was overwhelming, but Loki had no choice.

He approached a vendor selling newspapers.

"Excuse me," Loki said, holding up the envelope. "Do you recognize this postmark? Do you know where it might have come from?"

The vendor squinted at the envelope, then shook his head. "Could be from any of the drop boxes around here," he said. "There's one on the corner of 5th and Elm. Another near the bus station. Take your pick."

Loki thanked him and made his way to the first location.

The drop box on 5th and Elm was worn and rusted, its paint peeling in long, jagged strips. Loki stood in front of it, unsure what he was even looking for. He glanced around, hoping for a clue—a camera, a witness, anything.

A man leaning against the wall nearby caught his attention. He was older, his face weathered and lined, and he watched Loki with a curious expression.

"You lookin' for somethin'?" the man asked, his voice rough.

"Did you see anyone use this box recently?" Loki asked, showing him the envelope. "It would've been a few days ago."

The man scratched his chin. "Maybe. There's always people around here, droppin' off mail, but nothin' outta the ordinary. Why? Somethin' important?"

"My daughter..." Loki hesitated. He didn't know how much to reveal. "It's urgent, that's all."

The man nodded, his expression softening. "Try the bus station. People there notice more than they let on."

The bus station was a chaotic mess of people coming and going. Loki felt like a needle in a haystack, lost in the sea of faces. He approached the ticket counter, showing the clerk the envelope.

"Did you see anyone drop off a letter recently? Maybe someone acting suspicious?"

The clerk frowned, shaking her head. "Sorry, sir. I don't pay attention to that kind of thing."

Defeated, Loki wandered into the waiting area. He sat down on a worn bench, staring at the envelope in his hands.

"Looks like you're in a bind."

Loki turned to see a young woman sitting a few seats away, her dark hair pulled back in a messy bun. She had a sharpness in her eyes that suggested she noticed things most people didn't.

"I'm looking for someone," Loki said cautiously.

"Who isn't?" she replied with a smirk.

"It's my daughter. She's been... taken. I think whoever sent this envelope might have been here."

The woman's expression shifted. She leaned closer. "Taken? Like, kidnapped?"

Loki nodded.

She glanced at the envelope. "I don't recognize it, but there's a guy who hangs around here. Claims he sees everything. Calls himself Sparrow."

"Where can I find him?"

She pointed toward the back of the station, where a cluster of people stood smoking near the dumpsters.

Sparrow was easy to spot—a wiry man with a sharp face and eyes that darted around constantly, like a bird searching for prey. Loki approached him cautiously.

"You Sparrow?"

The man tilted his head, studying Loki. "Depends who's asking."

"I'm looking for someone. My daughter. She's been kidnapped, and I think the person who took her might've sent this from here." He showed Sparrow the envelope.

Sparrow snorted. "Kidnapped, huh? That's heavy. What's in it for me?"

Loki clenched his fists. "I don't have time for this. If you know something, tell me."

Sparrow smirked, clearly enjoying the power. "Relax, man. I might've seen someone. What's it worth to you?"

"I don't have money," Loki admitted. "But if you help me find her, I'll owe you. Whatever you want."

Sparrow considered this for a moment, then shrugged. "Alright. There was a guy here a few days ago, real twitchy. Kept looking over his shoulder, like he thought someone was watching him. Dropped off a letter at the box outside, then took off. Didn't look like the friendly type."

"Where did he go?"

"Caught a bus heading toward Redgate," Sparrow said. "That's all I know."

Redgate. The name sent a chill through Loki. It was a rundown industrial district on the edge of the city, a place where people went when they didn't want to be found.

By the time Loki reached Redgate, the sun was beginning to set. The district was as desolate as he remembered—empty warehouses, broken streetlights, and graffiti-covered walls.

He parked his car and stepped out, the hairs on the back of his neck standing on end. This was the kind of place where danger lurked around every corner.

He started walking, his eyes scanning the buildings for any sign of activity. Most were boarded up, their windows shattered, but one stood out. The door was slightly ajar, and a faint light flickered inside.

Loki approached cautiously, his heart pounding. He peered through the crack in the door, but the interior was too dark to see clearly.

Taking a deep breath, he pushed the door open and stepped inside.

The air was heavy with the smell of mildew and something else—something metallic. The flickering light came from a single bulb hanging from the ceiling, casting long shadows across the room.

Loki's footsteps echoed as he moved further inside. He was about to call out when he heard it: a faint noise, like a muffled cry.

"Lila?" he whispered, his voice trembling.

The sound stopped.

Loki's chest tightened as he moved toward the source of the noise. He reached a door at the back of the room and pressed his ear against it.

Nothing.

With shaking hands, he turned the knob and pushed the door open.

The room was empty.

CHAPTER NINE

THE FIRST SPARKS

The air in the room was thick, stale, as though it had been sealed off for years. Loki stood in the doorway, his eyes darting across the dimly lit space. A wooden table sat in the center, its surface worn and uneven, while a single chair lay toppled nearby. It didn't look like much, but something about the room felt off, as though it were holding its breath, waiting to reveal its secrets.

He approached the table slowly, the sound of his footsteps echoing in the stillness. On the surface lay an old notebook, its cover plain and unmarked, its edges frayed from age and use. Hesitant but desperate, Loki picked it up and flipped it open.

The pages were filled with scribbled handwriting, chaotic and fragmented. Most of it seemed nonsensical—arrows pointing to nothing, disconnected phrases, and markings that led nowhere. His frustration grew with every page, the hope that this might hold answers slipping further away.

And then, on one page, he found it. The words leapt out at him: "Redgate Pier – 47 – 11 p.m."

His heart pounded as he stared at the note. A time. A location. It had to mean something. Was this a meeting point? A clue to where they might have taken Lila? He couldn't be sure, but he knew he couldn't leave it behind. He slipped the notebook into his jacket pocket, the weight of it pressing against him like a promise.

As he turned away from the table, his eyes fell on the chair lying on its side. At first, it seemed as unremarkable as the rest of the room, but something made him pause. The legs of the chair were scratched, the marks deep and jagged, as though it had been dragged across the floor with force. He crouched down, his fingers brushing against the grooves in the concrete.

The scratches formed a faint trail, leading toward the far corner of the room. Loki followed it, his heart pounding louder with every step. The corner seemed empty at first, but as he crouched down to inspect it more closely, he noticed something unusual—a brick, slightly out of place in the wall.

He reached out, prying the loose brick free. Behind it was a crumpled piece of paper, hidden as if someone had left it there deliberately. Loki unfolded it carefully, the fragile paper threatening to tear under his touch.

The message scrawled on it was brief, but it sent a chill down his spine:

"She's scared. You need to hurry."

The words were rushed, the handwriting uneven. He read it over and over, trying to make sense of it. Who had written it? And why had they hidden it here?

Loki leaned back against the wall, the note trembling in his hands. His mind raced, piecing together everything he'd found—the notebook, the scratches, the hidden message. There was a connection, something just out of reach.

He closed his eyes, forcing himself to focus. He thought about the phone call, the distorted voice, the desperation in Lila's words. The pieces of the puzzle began to shift in his mind, rearranging themselves into something clearer.

Suddenly, his eyes snapped open. He shot to his feet, his heart pounding with a renewed sense of purpose.

He had an idea. A bright, daring idea.

But there was no time to waste.

CHAPTER TEN

THE PIER AT MIDNIGHT

The night was alive with sound: the hum of distant traffic, the whistle of a sharp wind threading through alleyways, the occasional bark of a stray dog. But for Loki, the world outside barely registered. His mind was a vortex of thoughts, his heart a drumbeat of urgency as he set his plan into motion.

He didn't stop to think twice, didn't let himself hesitate. He'd made a decision—a risky one—but hesitation was a luxury he couldn't afford. Every second that ticked away felt like a thread unraveling from the rope that tied him to Lila.

The first step was preparation. Loki returned to his small apartment, its familiar walls now a cold reminder of his responsibilities. He moved with purpose, grabbing items that seemed random to an outsider: a flashlight, duct tape, gloves, and an old, battered map of the city. He tossed them into his worn satchel, his hands trembling slightly as he zipped it shut.

He paused for a moment, his gaze drifting to the small photograph on the kitchen counter. It was a snapshot of him and Lila from years ago—her face alight with laughter, his arm wrapped protectively around her shoulders. He clenched his jaw, his fingers brushing the frame.

"I'll find you," he whispered, his voice breaking. "No matter what it takes."

Loki left the apartment, locking the door behind him with more force than necessary. The city stretched out before him, vast and unyielding, but he moved through it with a singular focus. He avoided the main streets, slipping into quieter paths and alleys, his figure a shadow among shadows.

His steps eventually led him to a neighborhood he hadn't visited in years. It was a part of the city he'd sworn to leave behind—a place where memories lingered like ghosts. But now, he had no choice. The plan demanded it.

A flickering streetlamp illuminated a battered iron gate ahead. Beyond it was a crumbling warehouse, its windows shattered, its walls scrawled with graffiti. Loki hesitated for a brief moment, his pulse quickening, before pushing the gate open. The metal screeched loudly, its protest echoing into the night.

Inside, the warehouse was a maze of debris and decay. Rusted machinery loomed like forgotten relics, their shadows stretching across the floor. Loki's flashlight beam cut through the darkness, sweeping across piles of discarded tools and broken crates. He moved quickly but carefully, his every step measured.

He stopped near a corner, crouching down to inspect a pile of old tarps. His hands moved deftly, searching for something beneath the layers. Finally, he found it: a hidden compartment in the floorboards. With a grunt, he pried it open, revealing a small, metallic case.

Loki opened the case, his eyes narrowing as he took inventory of its contents. It was all still there—everything he'd stashed away years ago, never expecting to need it again. A burner phone, a lock-picking kit, and a small, nondescript envelope. He pocketed the items quickly, his mind already racing ahead to the next step.

The plan wasn't linear. It wasn't simple. But it was the only chance he had.

He retraced his steps through the warehouse, pausing occasionally to check for signs that he was being followed. The kidnappers had been clever so far—taunting him, leaving just enough clues to keep him guessing. But Loki was determined to outsmart them.

His next destination was the Redgate Pier. The notebook's cryptic message had been clear about the location, but Loki wasn't heading there for answers just yet. He had another stop to make first—a place that might give him an edge.

The streets grew quieter as he approached the edge of the city. The buildings thinned out, replaced by empty lots and abandoned storefronts. Loki's grip on his satchel tightened as he entered a narrow alley, his senses on high alert.

At the end of the alley was a door, unmarked and unassuming. He knocked three times, his knuckles rapping against the peeling paint. There was a long pause, followed by the sound of locks clicking open.

The man who appeared in the doorway was older, his face lined with suspicion. He glanced at Loki, his eyes narrowing.

"Thought I'd never see you again," the man said, his voice gruff.

"Didn't think I'd have to come back," Loki replied, his tone steady but urgent. "I need your help."

The man sighed, stepping aside to let Loki in. Inside, the room was cluttered with tools, wires, and devices that hummed faintly with electricity. It was a makeshift workshop, the kind of place where no questions were asked.

Loki laid out his request quickly, speaking in low, measured tones. The man listened, nodding occasionally but saying little. When Loki finished, the man leaned back, crossing his arms.

"You're playing a dangerous game," he said. "You sure about this?"

"I don't have a choice," Loki said, his voice firm.

The man nodded again, then turned to the workbench, pulling together what Loki needed.

Hours later, Loki found himself standing at the edge of the pier, the cold wind biting at his face. The sea stretched out before him, dark and endless, its waves crashing against the wooden posts. He clutched the satchel tightly, his fingers numb from the chill.

He glanced at his watch. The time was approaching.

His mind raced with possibilities, doubts creeping in around the edges. But he pushed them aside, focusing instead on the clues he'd gathered and the steps he'd taken to get here.

He was ready.

Or at least, he had to be.

CHAPTER ELEVEN

THE TRAILS IN THE SHADOW

The wind howled across the pier, a low, mournful cry that seemed to echo Loki's unease. He stood motionless, staring out over the dark waters. Waves crashed against the wooden posts below, each splashes a stark reminder of the ticking clock in his mind. Somewhere out there, Lila was waiting, and every second that passed felt like an accusation: Why haven't you found her yet?

But Loki was not one to crumble under pressure. His plan was in motion, intricate and precarious, with no room for error. The clues he'd gathered so far were threads in a tangled web, and he was determined to follow each one to the end, no matter how dangerous the path.

From his vantage point, the pier stretched endlessly in both directions, a lonely expanse of decaying wood and rusted metal. The notebook's message—Redgate Pier, 47, 11 p.m.—had brought him here, but Loki knew better than to expect straightforward answers. If anything, the cryptic note felt more like bait, carefully laid to lure him into a trap.

He adjusted the strap of his satchel, the weight of its contents grounding him. Every item he'd packed was essential, chosen with the precision of someone who had planned for contingencies. Yet even with all his preparation, doubt gnawed at the edges of his resolve.

Loki moved cautiously along the pier, his boots making barely a sound against the worn planks. His flashlight cut through the darkness, revealing glimpses of scattered debris: an abandoned fishing net, a pile of shattered glass, a rusted anchor chain coiled like a sleeping serpent. Nothing out of the ordinary, nothing that screamed clue.

But Loki had learned to trust his instincts, and his instincts told him he was being watched.

He stopped abruptly, his flashlight beam resting on an old shipping container stacked haphazardly near the edge of the pier. The container was dented and weathered, its paint peeling in jagged strips. Loki approached it slowly, his hand brushing against the side as he walked its length.

At the far end, he found what he was looking for: a faint trail of mud leading from the container to the water's edge. It wasn't much, but it was enough to spark suspicion. Loki knelt, examining the ground more closely. The footprints were uneven, as though someone had been dragging a heavy object—or struggling to carry something unwilling.

He straightened, his heart pounding as he scanned the area. The footprints disappeared into the water, leaving him with more questions than answers.

"Think, Loki," he muttered to himself, his voice barely audible over the wind.

As he retraced his steps, Loki's thoughts turned to the message he'd found in the hidden compartment: "She's scared. You need to hurry." Who had written it? Was it someone trying to help him, or another ploy by the kidnappers to throw him off? The handwriting had been hurried, almost desperate, which didn't match the calculated coldness of the phone calls.

His thoughts were interrupted by the faint sound of metal scraping against metal. He froze, every muscle in his body tensing as he strained to pinpoint the source. It came again, faint but deliberate like a door being forced open.

Loki moved toward the sound, his flashlight guiding the way. The noise led him to another section of the pier, where a set of stairs descended into a maintenance area beneath the main structure. The air grew colder as he descended, the smell of saltwater and rust filling his nostrils.

The maintenance area was a labyrinth of steel beams and crisscrossing pipes, dimly lit by flickering bulbs that cast eerie shadows. Loki moved carefully, his footsteps muffled by the damp concrete.

As he rounded a corner, he saw it: a makeshift workstation, hastily assembled with a foldout table and a cluster of monitors powered by a humming generator. Wires snaked across the floor, connecting the monitors to a series of cameras and recording devices.

Loki's stomach clenched. The monitors displayed live feeds from various locations—dark alleys, abandoned buildings, and what appeared to be the interior of a van. He recognized none of the locations, but the implications were chilling. Someone had been watching, tracking movements, gathering information.

His attention was drawn to one particular feed: a dimly lit room with a single chair bolted to the floor. The chair was empty, but the sight of it sent a shiver down Loki's spine. He stepped closer, his eyes scanning the screen for any detail that might give him a clue.

Suddenly, one of the monitors flickered, the image shifting to static before displaying a new feed. This one was off the pier itself, taken from an angle high above. Loki felt his chest tighten as he realized what it meant—whoever had set this up knew he was there.

The sound of footsteps behind him shattered his concentration. He spun around, his flashlight beam catching the edge of a figure as it disappeared into the shadows.

"Who's there?" Loki called, his voice echoing in the confined space.

There was no response, only the faint echo of retreating steps. Loki clenched his jaw, his mind racing. He couldn't afford to lose whoever it was—they might be the key to finding Lila.

He took off after the figure, weaving through the maze of pipes and beams. The narrow pathways made it difficult to gain speed, but Loki pushed himself, his flashlight flickering as he rounded corner after corner.

The chase ended abruptly when Loki emerged into a wider area. The figure was gone, but the trail they'd left behind wasn't. A door stood ajar at the far end of the room, its edges smeared with fresh mud. Loki approached it cautiously, his hand on the doorknob.

The room beyond was small and empty, save for a single object lying in the centre of the floor: a familiar-looking scarf.

It was Lila's.

Loki's breath caught as he picked it up, the fabric still warm to the touch. His mind reeled with the implications. She had been here, possibly just moments ago.

As he stood there, clutching the scarf, a sound broke the silence—a faint beep, coming from somewhere nearby. Loki's eyes darted to the corner of the room, where a small device blinked with a steady red light.

It was a phone, and it was ringing.

A STEP FURTHER

The piercing ring of the phone echoed through the small, empty room, each beep drilling into Loki's mind like an unrelenting alarm. The scarf in his hand felt heavy, as though it carried the weight of a thousand unanswered questions. His instincts screamed at him to answer, but another voice in his head warned him to proceed carefully.

With trembling fingers, Loki picked up the phone, a cheap, outdated model that looked like it had been through years of wear and tear. The screen displayed nothing—no caller ID, no indication of who might be on the other end. He hesitated for a fraction of a second before pressing the green button and raising the phone to his ear.

A moment of silence passed, stretching thin like a taut wire. Then, a distorted voice crackled through the receiver, low and cold, dripping with malice.

"You're getting closer, Loki."

His blood ran cold.

"Who is this?" he demanded, his voice firm but edged with a tremor he couldn't suppress.

"You're asking the wrong questions," the voice replied, calm and calculating. "The right question is: how far are you willing to go?"

Loki's grip on the phone tightened, his knuckles turning white. "Tell me where she is."

A chuckle echoed through the line, hollow and devoid of warmth. "All in due time. But let me warn you—every step forward comes with a price. Are you prepared to pay it?"

Before Loki could respond, the line went dead. The abrupt silence left a void that seemed to press against him from all sides. He lowered the phone slowly, his mind racing.

Loki stepped out of the room, the cold night air hitting him like a slap. He tucked the scarf into his satchel, its presence a reminder of what was at stake. The message from the distorted voice was cryptic, but it only strengthened his resolve.

He retraced his steps back to the pier, scanning his surroundings for anything he might have missed earlier. The live camera feed in the maintenance area had been a chilling revelation, but it also gave him an idea: someone was watching him closely, which meant they might slip up if he kept moving.

The night deepened as Loki ventured further into the city. The streets were eerily quiet, the glow of streetlights casting long shadows across the pavement. He avoided the main thoroughfares, sticking to side alleys and backroads. The city's underbelly was a labyrinth of secrets, and Loki knew it better than most.

His next stop was a location he hadn't dared to visit in years: an underground club on the outskirts of town. The club, known as The Iron Veil, was infamous for its connections to the city's underworld. Loki had tangled with some of its patrons during his younger, more reckless days, but he hoped his past ties would work in his favor now.

The entrance to The Iron Veil was hidden behind an unmarked steel door in a nondescript alley. Loki knocked twice, paused, then knocked three more times—a signal that had once granted him entry. The door creaked open a fraction, revealing a pair of sharp, suspicious eyes.

"What do you want?" the man behind the door growled.

"Information," Loki said, his voice steady. "And I'm willing to pay for it."

The man studied him for a moment before stepping aside. Loki entered, the heavy door slamming shut behind him.

The club was as he remembered: dimly lit, smoke-filled, and teeming with unsavory characters. Conversations buzzed in hushed tones, deals were made in shadowy corners, and the air was thick with tension. Loki ignored the curious glances thrown his way as he made his way to the bar.

A woman with a no-nonsense demeanor and a scar running down her cheek greeted him. Her name was Mara, and she was the unofficial gatekeeper of The Iron Veil.

"Loki," she said, raising an eyebrow. "Didn't think I'd see your face again. What brings you here?"

"I need answers," Loki replied, leaning in so his voice wouldn't carry. "And I think you can help me."

Mara's eyes narrowed. "Depends on what you're asking. And how much you're willing to pay."

Loki slid a wad of cash across the bar. "Tell me about the cameras near Redgate Pier. Who's watching?"

Mara's expression didn't change, but Loki caught the flicker of recognition in her eyes. She hesitated for a moment before leaning closer.

"There's a group," she said in a low voice. "Calls themselves The Black Hounds. They've been operating in the shadows for years—kidnappings, extortion, you name it. If they've got their eyes on you, you're in deep."

Loki's stomach tightened. He had heard of The Black Hounds before, whispered rumors that painted them as ruthless and untouchable.

"Where do I find them?" he asked.

Mara shook her head. "You don't find them. They find you. But if you're looking for a lead..." She paused, glancing around before scribbling something on a napkin. "Try this address. It's not much, but it's the best I've got."

Loki took the napkin, his eyes scanning the hastily written words: 48 Mercy Street.

The address led Loki to an abandoned industrial complex on the outskirts of the city. The building loomed like a monolith, its windows shattered and its walls streaked with grime. Loki parked his car a safe distance away, his nerves taut as he approached the entrance.

The interior was a wasteland of rusted machinery and crumbling concrete. Loki moved cautiously, his flashlight cutting through the darkness. He searched every corner, every crevice, but the place seemed devoid of life.

Then he saw it: a faint glow emanating from a room at the end of a long corridor. His pulse quickened as he approached, his steps silent against the gritty floor. The glow grew brighter, and as Loki reached the doorway, he saw a desk covered in papers, maps, and photographs.

He scanned the room, his eyes falling on a single photograph pinned to the wall. It was of Lila, her face pale and frightened, her eyes wide with terror. Beneath the photograph was a message scrawled in red ink:

"You're running out of time."

Loki's breath caught as the weight of the situation pressed down on him. He didn't know how much longer he could hold himself together, but one thing was certain: he wasn't giving up. Not now. Not ever.

CHAPTER THIRTEEN

Loki stood in the dimly lit room, the photograph of Lila and the ominous message burning into his mind. His pulse thundered in his ears as his eyes swept over the desk again. The maps, papers, and scattered notes were a jumble of information, but they spoke volumes about the operation he was up against.

Whoever had taken Lila wasn't just toying with him—they were watching, controlling, and anticipating his every move.

He grabbed the papers and photographs, stuffing them into his satchel. Each piece of evidence might hold the key to finding her, and he wasn't leaving anything behind. As he turned to leave, a faint sound froze him in place.

A shuffle.

Someone else was in the building.

Loki extinguished his flashlight and moved silently toward the shadows. His heartbeat quickened, but his steps remained calculated and deliberate. He pressed his back against the cold concrete wall, peering around the corner.

There, at the far end of the corridor, a flicker of movement. A shadow stretched and shifted as faint footsteps echoed through the desolate structure.

Loki's instincts screamed for him to retreat, but he needed answers. Whoever was here might be connected to Lila's disappearance—or worse, they might be the ones orchestrating it.

He followed the sound, his body tense and his senses heightened. The building's labyrinthine layout worked against him; every hallway looked the same, and every creak of the floor beneath his feet seemed to betray his presence.

As he turned a corner, he saw the figure: a man in dark clothing, his back turned, seemingly inspecting a rusted door. Loki couldn't see his face, but the man's posture radiated authority.

"Who are you?" Loki demanded, stepping into view.

The man spun around, startled. For a moment, they locked eyes—a flicker of recognition in the stranger's gaze that made Loki's stomach drop.

"You're not supposed to be here," the man said, his voice steady but laced with tension.

"Neither are you," Loki shot back, taking a cautious step closer. "Where's my daughter?"

The man's expression didn't falter, but his hand moved toward his pocket. Loki reacted instinctively, closing the distance and grabbing the man's wrist before he could pull out whatever he was reaching for.

A struggle ensued, brief but intense. Loki wasn't as strong as he once was, but desperation gave him an edge. He slammed the man against the wall, pinning him with one arm while reaching into his pocket with the other.

His hand closed around a small device—a pager, outdated but functional. Loki yanked it free and stepped back, keeping his eyes locked on the man.

"What is this?" Loki demanded, holding up the pager.

The man smirked, blood trickling from a cut on his lip. "It's your next step. If you're brave enough to take it."

CHAPTER FOURTEEN

THE HUNT BEGINS(2)

The wind howled through the empty streets as Loki paced his small, dimly lit apartment. The weight of the text message lingered in his mind like a storm cloud.

"Clock's ticking."

It wasn't just a threat—it was a reminder of how little time he had left. He pulled out the collection of papers and photographs he had taken from the warehouse and spread them across his coffee table. Every detail, every word, every smudge on the paper could hold a clue.

His eyes fell on a map of the city with several locations marked in red. Most were places he recognized—warehouses, docks, abandoned buildings. They were all areas that could easily hide illegal activity. But one location stood out: Trinity Bridge.

Unlike the others, Trinity Bridge wasn't secluded or hidden. It was a busy part of the city, bustling with commuters and tourists. Why mark such a public place? Was it a misdirection, or did it hold a deeper significance?

Loki circled the location on the map and grabbed his coat. The bridge was as good a starting point as any.

The city was alive with activity as Loki approached Trinity Bridge. Cars zipped by, their headlights cutting through the darkness. Pedestrians moved in clusters, their laughter and chatter blending with the hum of traffic.

Loki kept his head low, his eyes scanning the faces of everyone he passed. He didn't know what he was looking for, but he trusted his instincts to guide him

As he reached the center of the bridge, he noticed a man leaning against the railing, his face obscured by a hood. The man's posture was casual, but there was something about him that made Loki's nerves stand on edge.

Loki approached cautiously, his footsteps muffled by the noise of the city. "Nice night," he said, testing the waters.

The man turned his head slightly, just enough for Loki to catch a glimpse of his face. It was the same man he had confronted at the warehouse.

"You're persistent," the man said, his voice carrying over the noise. "I'll give you that."

"Where is she?" Loki demanded, stepping closer.

The man chuckled. "Still asking the wrong questions. But since you've made it this far, I'll give you a hint."

He reached into his pocket and pulled out a small envelope, holding it out to Loki. "Take it. It's your next step."

Loki snatched the envelope and opened it, revealing a photograph of Lila tied to a chair in what appeared to be an old basement. Behind her, the wall was covered in graffiti—a swirling pattern of red and black that was unmistakable.

Loki's chest tightened. He knew that pattern. It was the symbol of an old gang that used to operate in the city: The Red Serpents.

Before Loki could react, the man stepped onto the railing and jumped over the side of the bridge. Loki rushed to the edge, but the man was gone, swallowed by the darkness below.

Back at his apartment, Loki spread the photograph out on the table and stared at the graffiti in the background. The Red Serpents hadn't been active for years, but their old hideout had been in a crumbling building on the east side of the city.

He pulled up a map on his phone and pinpointed the location: an abandoned factory near the river. It was risky, but Loki didn't care.

Every clue brought him closer to Lila.

The factory loomed like a ghost in the night, its silhouette jagged against the sky. Broken windows stared out like empty eyes, and the faint sound of dripping water echoed through the silence.

Loki moved cautiously, his flashlight slicing through the darkness. The air was thick with the smell of rust and decay, and every step he took stirred up clouds of dust.

He searched the first floor meticulously, checking every room and corner. Most of the space was filled with rusted machinery and piles of debris, but there was no sign of Lila.

As he climbed to the second floor, he noticed a faint glow coming from one of the rooms. His pulse quickened as he approached, the beam of his flashlight steady despite the tremor in his hand.

The room was empty, save for a single television screen mounted on the wall. As Loki stepped inside, the screen flickered to life, displaying a grainy video feed.

It was Lila.

She was still tied to the chair, her face pale and streaked with tears. Her head was bowed, and her breathing was shallow, but she was alive.

"Lila!" Loki shouted, his voice cracking.

The video feed cut out, replaced by a message in bold red letters: "You're close, Loki. Keep going."

Loki's fists clenched. Whoever was behind this wasn't just holding Lila—they were playing a game, and he was their pawn.

As he left the factory, his phone buzzed again. This time, the message was an address: 17 Ashwood Lane.

The name sent a chill down Loki's spine. Ashwood Lane was on the outskirts of the city, a place shrouded in urban legends and whispers of criminal activity. People rarely ventured there, and those who did often didn't return.

Loki climbed into his car, and the address burned into his memory. His determination burned brighter than ever, but so did his fear.

Lila's captors were leading him into the heart of their operation, and he had no choice but to follow.

Before Loki could respond, the man twisted free and bolted down the hallway. Loki chased after him, but the man was fast, disappearing into the maze of corridors.

Panting, Loki returned to the room, clutching the pager. The device was old but still functional, with a small screen that displayed a single message:

"Red River Dock. Midnight."

Loki's grip tightened. Another lead. Another step forward.

As midnight approached, Loki found himself standing at Red River Dock, the cold wind biting through his jacket. The docks were a sprawling expanse of shipping containers, cranes, and warehouses. The air smelled of salt and rust, and the only sounds were the distant lapping of water and the occasional groan of metal.

He kept to the shadows, his every sense on high alert. The message on the pager had been clear, but Loki didn't trust it. He knew he was being lured into a trap, but he had no choice—Lila's life was on the line.

As he moved through the maze of containers, he noticed faint markings on some of them: chalk symbols, barely visible in the darkness. They were simple shapes—circles, arrows, and crosses—but they seemed to form a trail.

Loki followed the markings cautiously, his footsteps silent against the concrete. The trail led him to a secluded area near the edge of the dock, where a single container stood apart from the rest. Its doors were slightly ajar, and a dim light spilt out from within.

He approached the container, his heart pounding. The light inside flickered, casting eerie shadows across the walls. Loki stepped inside, his breath hitching as he took in the scene.

The interior was empty, save for a single chair and a table. On the table lay a piece of paper, a small tape recorder, and a pair of handcuffs. The paper bore a short message, written in the same red ink as the one in the photograph:

"Sit. Listen. Wait."

Loki's hands trembled as he picked up the tape recorder. He pressed play, and the distorted voice from the phone call filled the air.

"Welcome, Loki," the voice said. "You're proving to be quite resourceful. But this is only the beginning."

The message continued, taunting him with cryptic hints and veiled threats. Loki's frustration boiled over, and he slammed the recorder onto the table, shattering it.

As he exited the container, his mind raced. The clues were piling up, but they still felt disjointed, like pieces of a puzzle with no clear picture. He needed to step back, to think, to regroup.

But as he turned to leave, his phone buzzed. Another message, this one simpler than the rest:

"Clock's ticking."

Loki stared at the screen, his resolve hardening. He didn't know who he was up against, but he wasn't going to let them win.

Whatever it took, wherever it led—he would find Lila.

CHAPTER FIFTEEN

The city lights blurred in Loki's rearview mirror as he sped toward Ashwood Lane. His grip on the steering wheel was tight, his knuckles white. The air in the car was heavy with the weight of his determination, fear, and desperation. The address burned in his mind like a brand: 17 Ashwood Lane.

The roads grew quieter as he left the bustling core of the city. Streetlights became fewer, their flickering bulbs barely illuminating the cracked pavement. The buildings in this part of town were in various states of disrepair, their broken windows and graffiti-covered walls standing as a testament to neglect and decay.

Loki's heart raced as he approached the turnoff to Ashwood Lane. The street was shrouded in shadow, with only the faint glow of the moon to guide him. He slowed the car and parked a block away, unwilling to alert anyone to his presence.

With a deep breath, Loki stepped out of the car and into the frigid night air. He pulled his jacket tighter around himself and began to walk, his footsteps muffled by the uneven asphalt. Every sound—every creak, every whisper of the wind—felt magnified in the silence.

As he approached the address, his eyes scanned the surrounding buildings for any sign of movement. Ashwood Lane was eerily quiet, the kind of quiet that pressed against your chest and made it hard to breathe.

When he reached the corner of the street, he spotted it: a black van parked in front of an abandoned warehouse. The van was unmarked, its windows tinted so dark that even moonlight couldn't penetrate them.

Loki's instincts flared. This was it.

He pressed himself against the wall of a nearby building and watched as two men emerged from the van. They were dressed in dark clothing, their faces obscured by scarves. One of them carried a small duffel bag, its weight evident by the way he held it.

Loki's heart pounded as he followed them from a distance, his steps careful and deliberate. The men moved with purpose, their voices low as they exchanged a few words.

They entered the warehouse through a side door, leaving it slightly ajar. Loki crept closer, his breaths shallow and controlled. He reached the door and peered inside, his eyes adjusting to the dim interior.

The warehouse was a cavernous space, its walls lined with rusted machinery and stacks of wooden crates. The air smelled of oil and mildew, and the faint sound of dripping water echoed through the emptiness. Loki slipped inside, his movements careful to avoid making noise.

He stayed in the shadows, watching as the two men disappeared through another door at the far end of the room. Loki waited for a moment before following, his heart pounding with every step.

The second room was smaller, with a table in the center and a few folding chairs scattered around. A single light bulb hung from the ceiling, casting a harsh glow over the scene.

On the table lay a stack of papers and what looked like a small, outdated radio. Loki's eyes scanned the room, but there was no sign of Lila.

As he crept closer to the table, his attention was drawn to a map pinned to the wall. It was a map of the city, with several locations marked in red. His eyes zeroed in on one of the marks—it was the same location as 17 Ashwood Lane.

Before he could examine it further, a noise behind him made him freeze.

He turned slowly, his body tense. A group of men stood at the entrance to the room, their faces shadowed but their postures unmistakably hostile. They were dressed in mismatched clothing, but what caught Loki's attention was the weapons they carried.

Metal rods, chains, and even a few crowbars gleamed in the dim light. The leader, a tall man with a scar running down his cheek, stepped forward.

"Well, well," the man said, his voice dripping with menace. "Looks like we've got ourselves a trespasser."

Loki's mind raced. These weren't the same men he had followed—this was a gang. And from the way they looked at him, they had no intention of letting him leave unscathed.

"I'm just passing through," Loki said, raising his hands in a gesture of surrender.

The leader chuckled, a sound that sent chills down Loki's spine. "Wrong place, wrong time, friend. And now you're gonna pay for it."

The men began to close in, their weapons tapping against the ground as they advanced. Loki's heart hammered in his chest as he backed away, his mind scrambling for a way out.

But the gang had already formed a circle, cutting off any chance of escape.

As the leader raised his rod, ready to strike, Loki's instincts kicked in. He dove to the side, narrowly avoiding the blow, and scrambled to his feet.

"Get him!" one of the men shouted, and chaos erupted.

CHAPTER SIXTEEN

The cold night air stung Loki's face as he sprinted through the dimly lit streets of Ashwood Lane. His breaths came in sharp, ragged gasps, each step pounding against the cracked asphalt. Behind him, the gang's shouts grew louder, their footsteps like thunder in the silence of the desolate area.

"Don't let him get away!" a voice bellowed, its rage cutting through the night.

Loki's heart pounded in his chest as he turned sharply down an alley, hoping to lose them in the maze of abandoned buildings. The shadows stretched long and menacing around him, and the narrow passageway felt suffocating.

But no matter how fast he ran, they were always just behind him, their determination relentless. His lungs burned, his legs screamed for rest, but he couldn't stop—not yet.

As he rounded another corner, he stumbled, his foot catching on a piece of debris. He hit the ground hard, his palms scraping against the rough pavement. For a moment, he lay there, dazed, the sounds of the gang growing closer.

"Got you now, hero," the leader's voice sneered as they caught up to him.

Loki tried to push himself up, but before he could, a sharp pain exploded in his side as the first blow landed.

They descended on him like a pack of wolves, their weapons swinging with brutal force. The clang of metal against flesh and bone echoed in the alley, mixing with Loki's cries of pain. He tried to shield himself, curling into a ball, but it was no use.

Each strike felt like fire, searing through his body. The world blurred around him, his vision fading in and out as the beating continued. Blood dripped from a gash on his forehead, pooling beneath him on the cold ground.

"Thought you could mess with us?" the leader growled, his voice venomous. "You're nothing, you hear me? Nothing!"

Loki tried to respond, but the words wouldn't come. His body felt heavy, his limbs numb. He didn't know how long it lasted—seconds, minutes, hours. Time lost all meaning in the haze of pain.

Finally, the blows stopped.

"Throw him in the river," someone said.

"No," the leader replied. "Let him suffer."

Two of the gang members grabbed Loki by the arms and dragged him out of the alley. His head lolled to the side, his swollen eyes catching fleeting glimpses of the night sky. The stars looked so distant, so unreachable.

They dumped him by the riverbank, his body landing with a dull thud in the damp grass. Loki tried to move, to call out, but his voice was a whisper lost to the wind.

"Let's go," the leader said, and their footsteps faded into the night.

Loki lay there, the world around him silent except for the gentle lapping of the river against the shore. The cold seeped into his bones, but he couldn't feel it fully through the numbness.

The memories of the past days flooded his mind—Lila's laughter, her bright eyes, the way she used to cling to his arm when she was scared.

He had failed her.

Tears mixed with the blood on his face as he stared up at the sky. For the first time in years, he prayed—prayed for the strength to get back up, to keep fighting, to bring her home.

And then, everything went dark.

When Loki opened his eyes, the blinding white light of a hospital room greeted him. The sterile smell of disinfectant filled his nostrils, and the steady beeping of a heart monitor echoed in his ears.

His body felt like it was made of lead, every movement sending waves of pain through him. His hands were bandaged, his ribs tightly wrapped, and his left eye was swollen shut.

"Good, you're awake," a nurse said, stepping into the room. Her face was kind, but there was a hint of pity in her eyes.

CHAPTER SEVENTEEN

MEMORIES OF THE LIGHT

Loki stared at the ceiling of the hospital room, his vision blurring as exhaustion and pain weighed on him. The steady beep of the heart monitor filled the silence, but he barely heard it. His mind was elsewhere, drifting back to a time when life was simpler, warmer, and whole.

It was Lila's laughter that came to him first. That bright, uninhibited giggle that had always filled their home. He could see her now in his mind's eye—her tiny hands clutching a crayon as she scribbled colorful streaks across a sheet of paper. She was only four then, her hair tied in two uneven pigtails that her mother had hastily put together before rushing out the door to work.

"You're drawing a masterpiece, Lila," he had said, crouching beside her on the living room floor.

"It's us!" she had exclaimed, her little finger pointing at a row of stick figures.

There was one with curly hair and a big smile—that was her. Another, taller figure with glasses—that was him. And in the middle, holding their hands, was Sarah, his wife, with her long hair flowing like a waterfall.

The memory made his chest tighten. Sarah had been the glue that held them together, a force of nature who could light up a room with just a smile. He remembered how she would hum as she prepared dinner, swaying slightly to the tune as she stirred a pot or chopped vegetables.

"Loki, taste this," she would say, holding out a spoon of steaming broth.

"It's perfect," he'd reply, even if it wasn't, because the truth was, anything Sarah made was perfect to him.

Their home had been filled with love, with life. Weekends were spent in the park, watching Lila climb the monkey bars and cheering her on like she was an Olympic athlete. Evenings were for board games and movie nights, the three of them huddled under a blanket on the couch.

Loki remembered the way Lila would fall asleep halfway through the movie, her head resting on his shoulder, her tiny hand clutching his shirt.

"She's just like you," Sarah would whisper, brushing a strand of hair from Lila's face.

"How so?" he'd ask.

"Stubborn, determined, and completely unaware of how much she's loved."

Tears slipped down Loki's cheeks as the memories overwhelmed him. How had it all gone so wrong?

The sound of rain tapping against the hospital window brought him back to the present. He turned his head, staring at the darkened city outside. Somewhere out there, his little girl was alone, scared, and waiting for him.

But why?

Why had someone taken her?

The question gnawed at him, its answer just out of reach. He had no enemies, no one who would have reason to hurt him or his family. Was it random? A cruel twist of fate?

Or was it something else?

His thoughts drifted to the people who had taken her. Who were they? What kind of monsters would steal a child from her father? He clenched his fists, his bandaged hands trembling.

But then another thought struck him—a thought he hated himself for having.

What if they weren't monsters?

What if they were desperate? What if they were people like him, struggling to make ends meet, doing whatever they could to survive?

He thought about the ransom demand. $50,000. It was an impossible amount for someone like him, but to the kidnappers, it might mean life or death.

Were they parents? Was there a little girl waiting for them at home, hungry and cold?

Loki's mind spiraled with possibilities. He imagined a woman crying as she told her husband they couldn't afford food that week. He pictured a father looking at his empty wallet, the weight of failure crushing him.

Was that what had driven them to this? Desperation?

But then, another image surfaced—Lila, her tear-streaked face, her big, frightened eyes.

He couldn't afford to think like this. Whatever their reasons, they had taken his daughter, and that was unforgivable. Desperation didn't excuse cruelty.

Loki's jaw tightened. He wouldn't let himself be consumed by sympathy for people who had torn his world apart. But the questions lingered, haunting him like ghosts.

Who were they? Why Lila?

And then, a darker thought crept in.

What if it wasn't about money? What if the ransom was a distraction, a cover for something far more sinister?

Loki shook his head, trying to banish the thought. He couldn't go down that road. Not yet.

As the first rays of dawn began to creep through the hospital window, Loki forced himself to stop.

He couldn't afford to lose himself in questions and what-ifs. He needed to focus, to be strong, to keep moving forward.

For Lila.

Loki tried to speak, but his throat was dry, the words catching like sandpaper. The nurse brought him a glass of water, holding it to his lips as he drank.

"You were lucky," she said softly. "Someone found you by the river and called an ambulance. You've been unconscious for two days."

Two days.

The words hit him like a hammer. Two days lost, two days that Lila was still out there, alone and terrified.

"Where... where's my daughter?" he croaked, his voice barely audible.

The nurse hesitated. "I don't know, sir. But you need to rest. You're in no condition to—"

"I have to find her," Loki interrupted, his voice stronger now despite the pain. He tried to sit up, but the sharp agony in his ribs forced him back down.

"Please," he begged, his eyes filling with tears. "She's all I have."

The nurse placed a gentle hand on his shoulder. "You'll get through this," she said, though her voice wavered.

As the hours passed, Loki lay in the hospital bed, his mind racing. The memory of the gang's taunts replayed over and over, their laughter echoing in his ears. He clenched his fists, ignoring the sting of the stitches on his palms.

He had come too far to give up now. Lila was waiting for him, and he would move heaven and earth to bring her back.

The pain in his body was nothing compared to the ache in his heart.

As night fell, Loki stared out the window at the city lights in the distance. Somewhere out there, his daughter was waiting for him. And no matter how broken he was, he would find her.

ALLIES IN THE SHADOWS

Loki leaned back against the pillows, the dull ache in his ribs reminding him of his vulnerability. He hated feeling this helpless, tied to the confines of the hospital bed while every fiber of his being screamed at him to be out there, searching for Lila.

He stared at the ceiling, racking his brain for ways to investigate without leaving the room. There had to be something—anything—he could do to keep the search moving forward. His thoughts were interrupted by the sound of footsteps approaching.

"Knock, knock," a familiar voice called.

Loki turned his head to see his three closest friends entering the room. Max, the sharp-witted journalist with a knack for digging up information, led the way. Behind him were Ian, the no-nonsense former cop turned private investigator, and Nate, the tech-savvy genius who could hack his way into anything.

"Loki, you look like hell," Max said with a grin, though his eyes betrayed genuine concern.

"Good to see you too," Loki replied, his voice dry.

Ian placed a bag of takeout on the side table. "Figured you might need some real food. Hospital stuff isn't exactly gourmet."

"And I brought this," Nate said, holding up a tablet. "Thought you might want to keep busy."

Loki couldn't help but smile. Despite the weight on his shoulders, seeing his friends brought a sense of relief he hadn't felt in days.

After some small talk and a half-hearted attempt to eat, Max finally asked the question that had been hanging in the air.

"Where's Lila, Loki?"

The room fell silent. Loki's throat tightened as he tried to find the words. He glanced at the floor, then back at his friends, their faces etched with worry.

"She's been taken," he said finally, his voice barely above a whisper.

The weight of the statement hung heavily in the room. Max leaned forward, his expression serious. Ian crossed his arms, his jaw tightening. Nate looked stunned, his usual easygoing demeanor replaced by quiet intensity.

"Taken?" Ian asked, his voice low but firm.

Loki nodded, then explained everything—the ransom demand, the chase through the streets, the gang that had beaten him and left him for dead.

"They want $50,000," Loki finished. "I don't have that kind of money. And even if I did, I don't trust them to let her go."

Max was the first to speak. "We'll find her, Loki. You know we will."

Ian nodded. "Whatever it takes. They messed with the wrong person."

Loki looked at them, gratitude and desperation warring in his eyes. "I need your help," he said, his voice breaking. "I can't do this alone."

"We're here," Nate said firmly.

"Anything you need," Max added.

Loki took a deep breath, then began outlining his plan.

"I need you to retrace my steps," he said. "Start where I was last attacked. Look for anything—any clues that could lead us to Lila or the people who took her."

Ian frowned. "What about the police? They might have missed something, but if we get too involved—"

"No police," Loki interrupted. "They'll only slow us down. We don't have time for bureaucracy."

Ian held his gaze for a moment, then nodded. "All right. We'll do it your way."

Nate tapped on his tablet. "I'll pull up maps of the area and see if there are any surveillance cameras nearby. Maybe we can get a lead that way."

"And I'll start asking around," Max said. "See if any of my sources have heard anything about a gang operating in that area."

The three of them left the hospital shortly after, each with their assignments. Loki watched them go, a mixture of hope and dread filling his chest.

Hours passed as Loki waited for updates, his mind racing with possibilities. He couldn't shake the image of Lila's frightened face, nor could he silence the nagging doubt that he wasn't doing enough.

Finally, his phone buzzed. It was Ian.

"We're here," Ian said, his voice steady but tense.

"Where?" Loki asked.

"At the place you described—the alley where you were attacked," Ian replied. "We're going in now. I'll let you know if we find anything."

"Be careful," Loki said, his grip tightening on the phone.

"We will," Ian assured him before the line went dead.

As Ian, Max, and Nate stood at the entrance to the dark alley, they exchanged uneasy glances. The place was eerily quiet, the kind of silence that made your skin crawl. The faint glow of a streetlight illuminated the graffiti-covered walls and broken glass littering the ground.

"This is it," Max said, his voice low.

"Let's see what we can find," Ian replied, stepping forward.

They moved cautiously, their eyes scanning every inch of the alley for clues. Ian's years of experience as a cop kicked in as he examined the ground, looking for any signs of a struggle. Max took photos of the area, while Nate used his tablet to scan for nearby devices that might have been connected to security cameras.

"What are we even looking for?" Max asked after a few minutes.

"Anything that doesn't belong," Ian said.

Nate knelt down, picking up a small piece of metal from the ground. "This could be something," he said, holding it up.

Ian frowned. "It's a start."

The deeper they went, the more the atmosphere shifted. There was something about the place—something sinister that none of them could quite put into words.

As they reached the spot where Loki had described being beaten, Ian's phone buzzed with a notification. He glanced at it, then back at Max and Nate.

"This is where it happened," he said quietly.

They all stood there for a moment, the weight of the situation sinking in.

"Let's keep looking," Ian said finally, his voice determined.

And with that, they stepped deeper into the shadows.

CHAPTER NINETEEN

ECHOES OF THE PAST

The alley was darker than the night itself, the air thick with a damp, metallic smell that clung to their senses. Ian led the way, his flashlight cutting through the murky shadows. Max followed closely, his camera ready to capture anything that might serve as a clue. Nate, with his ever-present tablet in hand, occasionally glanced at its screen, hoping for a breakthrough.

"This place gives me the creeps," Max muttered, his voice barely above a whisper.

"You're not alone," Nate replied, his eyes darting around. "Feels like something out of a horror movie."

"Focus," Ian said sharply, his tone brooking no nonsense. "We're here to find answers, not jump at shadows."

But even Ian, the hardened former cop, couldn't deny the unease crawling up his spine. The alley seemed to stretch endlessly, its jagged walls closing in on them the further they went.

They searched meticulously, their eyes combing every inch of the grimy ground and graffiti-covered walls. Ian paused to examine a rusty pipe lying in a corner, its surface stained with something dark. Max crouched near a pile of discarded cardboard, sifting through the debris with a grimace.

"Nothing," he said after a while, standing and dusting off his hands.

Nate glanced up from his tablet. "There aren't any active cameras in this area. If there were, they're long gone."

"Keep looking," Ian said, his voice firm.

As they ventured deeper into the alley, the oppressive silence was broken only by the sound of their footsteps and the occasional drip of water from somewhere above. The air grew colder, and a faint, musty odor began to permeate the area.

"What's that smell?" Max asked, covering his nose.

"Rot," Ian said grimly.

They turned a corner and stumbled upon something that made them freeze in their tracks.

There, in the dim light of Ian's flashlight, was a large, weathered board nailed to the wall. Its surface was covered with faded photographs, yellowed newspaper clippings, and scribbled notes. The images were gruesome—pictures of lifeless bodies sprawled in various states of decay, each more horrifying than the last.

"What the hell is this?" Nate whispered, his voice trembling.

Max stepped closer, his camera flashing as he captured the scene. "This... this is like some kind of murder shrine."

Ian's jaw tightened as he studied the board. The photographs weren't random. Each one depicted a different crime scene, and the victims all appeared to be tied to notorious murders that had made headlines years ago.

"Wait a second," Ian said, leaning in. "I recognize some of these cases."

"Me too," Max added, his brow furrowing. "These were all big stories back in the day. Serial killers, high-profile murders... These were the ones that shook the city."

Nate pointed to a piece of paper tacked to the center of the board. It was a crude map, hand-drawn with red Xs marking various locations.

"These must be where the bodies were found," he said.

Ian nodded, his expression grim. "Someone went to a lot of trouble to document this."

Max flipped through his mental archive of crime stories, trying to piece together the connections. "This doesn't make sense. Why would something like this be here? What does it have to do with Lila?"

Nate glanced nervously around the alley. "You think whoever made this is still around?"

Ian didn't answer immediately. He was too focused on a particular photograph near the bottom of the board. It showed a young woman lying on a concrete floor, her hands bound and her eyes staring blankly at the ceiling.

"She looks familiar," Ian muttered.

Max leaned over his shoulder. "She was one of the victims of the 'Riverbank Killer.' Remember? That guy who was never caught."

Ian nodded slowly. "Yeah, I remember. He left his victims near riversides, just like where Loki was found."

A chill ran down Nate's spine as he connected the dots. "You don't think... Could this have something to do with that? With the Riverbank Killer?"

"Too early to say," Ian said, though his voice was tinged with unease.

Max continued scanning the board, his eyes landing on a set of numbers scrawled in red ink. "What's this?" he asked, pointing.

"Coordinates, maybe?" Nate suggested, typing them into his tablet.

The screen blinked, then displayed a location on the outskirts of the city.

"It's a storage facility," Nate said, frowning. "Looks abandoned."

Ian's mind raced as he processed the information. "If this is connected to the kidnappers, it could be a lead. But why would they leave something like this behind?"

"Maybe they didn't," Max said. "Maybe this is their work. Or maybe someone else is trying to send a message."

As they continued examining the board, a sound broke the stillness—a faint rustling, like footsteps on gravel.

"Did you hear that?" Nate whispered, his eyes wide.

Ian held up a hand, signaling for silence. He turned off his flashlight, plunging them into darkness.

The three of them stood motionless, their breaths shallow as they strained to hear.

The rustling grew louder, then stopped.

"Let's get out of here," Max said, his voice barely audible.

"Not yet," Ian replied. "We need more information."

"But what if someone's watching us?" Nate asked, his voice shaking.

"Then we move carefully," Ian said.

They continued their search, their movements cautious and deliberate. The unease in the air was palpable, every shadow seeming to hide unseen eyes.

Finally, after what felt like hours, they stepped back to take in the board one last time.

"We need to show this to Loki," Max said.

"Agreed," Ian said. "But first, we need to figure out what all of this means."

As they turned to leave, Nate glanced over his shoulder one last time. The board seemed to stare back at him, its macabre contents a stark reminder of the darkness they were delving into.

The three of them exited the alley, their minds racing with questions and possibilities.

And somewhere in the shadows, unseen by them, a figure watched silently as they disappeared into the night.

CHAPTER TWENTY

THE UNVEILING

Loki sat upright in his hospital bed, his gaze locked on the disturbing photos Ian had just handed him. The images of crime scenes and murder victims were chilling, but it was the context behind them that unsettled him the most.

"Why would these people kidnap Lila?" Loki muttered, his voice filled with frustration. "I haven't done anything to anyone... I've kept to myself, worked hard, and minded my own business."

Max leaned against the window, his arms crossed. "Maybe it's not about you, Loki. Maybe it's about Lila."

Loki froze, his mind racing. "Lila?" he asked, incredulous. "She's just a teenager. What could she have possibly done to provoke something like this?"

Ian spoke up. "Teenagers can sometimes attract the wrong kind of attention without realizing it. It doesn't mean she's at fault, but it's worth looking into."

Nate, sitting on the chair by the bed, tapped at his tablet. "You said she was close to a couple of friends, right? Maybe they know something."

Loki hesitated, his thoughts swirling. The idea that Lila might have been involved in something dangerous was unbearable. But if there was even a chance it could lead to her, he had to know.

After a moment of deliberation, Loki pulled out his phone and dialed the number of one of Lila's close friends, Mia. It rang twice before a soft, hesitant voice answered.

"Hello?"

"Mia, it's Mr. Sørensen," Loki said, trying to keep his tone steady. "I need to talk to you about Lila. It's important."

There was a pause on the other end before Mia replied, "Is she okay?"

Loki's throat tightened. "No, she's not. She's missing, and I need your help to figure out what happened."

"I'll come right away," Mia said.

Loki then called Lila's other friend, Sophie, who agreed to join Mia.

An hour later, Mia and Sophie arrived at the hospital, their faces pale and anxious. Loki introduced them to Ian, Max, and Nate, then got straight to the point.

"Has Lila mentioned anything unusual to you?" Loki asked, his eyes scanning their faces. "Anything at all? Did she have any conflicts or problems with anyone recently?"

The girls exchanged nervous glances.

"Mia? Sophie?" Loki pressed gently.

"Well..." Mia began, fidgeting with her hands. "There was this one incident... but I don't think it's connected."

"What incident?" Loki asked, his voice sharpening.

Sophie hesitated. "It happened a few months ago. Lila and I were hanging out at the park, and these boys—four of them—started bothering us. They were saying nasty things, trying to scare us."

Mia nodded. "They wouldn't leave us alone, so Lila stood up to them."

"She slapped one of them," Sophie added.

Loki's heart sank. "She what?"

"She slapped him," Mia repeated, her voice trembling. "They were being awful, and Lila had enough. She told them to back off, and when they didn't, she hit one of them across the face. Hard."

"Did she know who they were?" Max asked, his journalist instincts kicking in.

The girls shook their heads.

"No," Sophie said, "but we found out later. They're the sons of a powerful guy—some kind of mafia leader. We didn't know at the time. We just thought they were some spoiled rich kids."

Loki felt a chill run down his spine. "A mafia leader?"

Mia nodded. "Yeah. After that day, they didn't come near us again, but... I don't know, Mr. Sørensen. What if this is about that?"

Ian, who had been silent until now, spoke up. "If those boys are connected to a mafia, it's possible they held a grudge. Even something as small as a slap could be seen as a blow to their pride, especially if their father is dangerous."

"But that was months ago," Loki argued, his voice rising. "Why wait until now?"

"Maybe they waited for the right moment," Max suggested. "Or maybe this isn't just about revenge. They could have ulterior motives."

Loki leaned back, his hands covering his face. The thought of his daughter being targeted because of a moment of bravery was unbearable.

Nate broke the silence. "We need more information on those boys. Names, backgrounds, anything we can use to track them down."

"I don't know their names," Mia admitted. "But they were always hanging around the park. Maybe someone there knows them."

Ian nodded. "It's a lead. We'll start there."

"Thank you," Loki said to the girls, his voice thick with emotion. "I know this isn't easy for you, but you've helped more than you know."

Mia and Sophie exchanged glances, then nodded.

"We just want Lila back," Sophie said softly.

After the girls left, Loki and his friends huddled together, strategizing their next move.

"If those boys are involved, this just got a lot more dangerous," Ian said.

"We'll tread carefully," Max replied. "But we can't back down now."

Nate tapped on his tablet, already searching for connections between the park and known mafia activity. "If they're the sons of a mafia leader, they've probably left some kind of trail. I'll dig into local crime reports and see what I can find."

"And we'll head to the park," Ian said. "See if anyone there remembers those boys."

Loki nodded, his resolve hardening. "We're getting closer. I can feel it."

But as they prepared to take their next steps, a sense of foreboding lingered in the air. The pieces of the puzzle were falling into place, but the picture they were forming was darker than any of them had anticipated.

CHAPTER TWENTY-ONE

THREADS IN THE DARKNESS

The next morning, Ian and Max prepared to visit the park while Nate stayed behind, glued to his tablet, meticulously scanning through online records and archived reports. Loki, still confined to his hospital bed, felt the sting of helplessness clawing at him. He wanted to be out there with them, pounding the pavement, demanding answers. But his battered body refused to cooperate, forcing him to trust his friends to act in his stead.

Ian adjusted his coat as he glanced at Max. "You ready for this?"

Max slung his camera over his shoulder. "As ready as I'll ever be. Let's hope the park jogs someone's memory."

The park was a stark contrast to the grim events unfolding in Loki's life. Children laughed and played, parents chatted on benches, and joggers moved rhythmically along the paths. The scene was tranquil, almost mocking in its normalcy.

Ian and Max began their search by speaking to the regulars—vendors selling ice cream, an elderly man feeding pigeons, a group of mothers gathered near the playground.

"Excuse me," Ian said to one of the mothers, flashing a polite smile. "I'm looking for information about a group of boys who used to hang out here a few months ago. Four of them, teenagers, probably from wealthy families."

The woman frowned, shaking her head. "I'm sorry, I don't recall anything like that."

They moved on to the ice cream vendor, an older man with sharp eyes.

"Teenagers?" the vendor repeated, stroking his chin. "Yeah, I remember a group of boys like that. Trouble, those ones. Always loud, always picking on people."

Max leaned in. "Do you know their names?"

The vendor shook his head. "No, but they had this air about them—like they thought they owned the place. I remember one of them had a scar on his cheek. Looked like he'd been in a fight."

Ian noted this down. "Do you remember the last time you saw them?"

"Not exactly, but they stopped coming around a while back. Can't say I missed them."

They continued asking around, piecing together fragmented descriptions of the boys. One had a penchant for flashy watches, another always carried a backpack, and a third was known for his loud, mocking laugh. The details were vague, but they painted a picture of a group used to getting their way through intimidation.

As they were about to leave, a young man approached them. He was thin, with a hoodie pulled low over his face.

"I heard you asking about those kids," he said, his voice low.

Ian and Max exchanged a glance.

"What do you know about them?" Ian asked.

"They're bad news," the man replied. "They used to hang out at that old billiard hall on Fifth Street. Everyone knows it's a front for something shady. If they're involved, you're dealing with more than just some spoiled brats."

Max jotted down the address. "Thanks. You've been a big help."

The man nodded and disappeared as quickly as he had come.

While Ian and Max were gathering intel, Loki was deep in conversation with Nate.

"I can't just sit here," Loki said, frustration lacing his voice. "I need to know who these people are."

"I'm working on it," Nate assured him, his fingers flying across his tablet's screen. "But it's not easy. The mafia doesn't exactly leave a digital footprint."

Loki stared out the window, his mind racing. He thought about the boys Mia and Sophie had described—the arrogance, the cruelty. But more than that, he thought about Lila's bravery. She had stood up to them, not for herself, but for her friends.

"She's strong," Loki said quietly.

Nate glanced up. "What?"

"Lila," Loki repeated. "She's strong. She always has been. Even when her mother passed, she held it together better than I did."

Nate nodded, unsure of what to say.

When Ian and Max returned, they relayed everything they had learned to Loki and Nate.

"A billiard hall on Fifth Street," Ian said. "It's worth checking out."

"Definitely," Nate agreed. "But we need to be careful. If it's connected to the mafia, walking in there unprepared could be dangerous."

"Ian and I will handle it," Max said. "You two stay here and keep working on the background."

Loki clenched his fists. "I hate being stuck here."

"You're doing your part, Loki," Ian said firmly. "Let us handle the legwork."

Ian and Max arrived at the billiard hall late in the evening. The building was dimly lit, its neon sign flickering intermittently. Inside, the atmosphere was thick with cigarette smoke and the sound of clacking pool balls.

They approached the bar, where a burly man with a shaved head stood wiping down glasses.

"We're looking for someone," Ian said, sliding a photo of the boys across the counter. "Recognize them?"

The man barely glanced at the photo before shaking his head. "Never seen 'em."

Max sighed. "We know they used to hang out here. We just need a name or a lead. Help us out, and we'll be on our way."

The bartender glared at them. "I said I don't know them. Now finish your drinks or get out."

Ian's jaw tightened, but he backed off, knowing they wouldn't get anything by pushing.

As they were leaving, Max spotted something—a graffiti tag on the wall outside the building. It matched a symbol they had seen on the board of photos in the alley.

"Look at this," Max said, pointing.

Ian frowned. "It's the same symbol. Whoever put that board together must have been here."

They photographed the graffiti and headed back, determined to follow the lead.

CHAPTER TWENTY-TWO

THE CALL THAT CHANGED EVERYTHING

The stillness in the hospital room was heavy, broken only by the faint hum of machines monitoring Loki's condition. The weight of the past few days pressed down on him like an unbearable burden. Every moment without Lila felt like a lifetime, and though his friends had been tirelessly working to uncover leads, Loki felt increasingly helpless.

Nate sat at a small desk in the corner, engrossed in his laptop. His headphones were around his neck, his brows furrowed in intense concentration. The room's dim lighting reflected off his glasses as lines of code scrolled across the screen.

"Any updates from Ian or Max?" Loki asked, his voice rough with exhaustion.

"Not yet," Nate replied without looking up. "They're still following up on the graffiti lead. But I've been scanning for any digital breadcrumbs left by the people who contacted you earlier."

Loki sighed, leaning back into his pillows. He hated feeling like a passive participant in this nightmare. He wanted to be out there, searching, pushing, doing something.

The sharp ring of the phone startled them both. Loki's pulse quickened as he grabbed it, his hand trembling slightly.

"Hello?" he said, trying to keep his voice steady.

For a moment, there was silence. Then a deep, distorted voice came through, sending a chill down Loki's spine.

"Mr. Lars," the voice drawled, slow and deliberate. "It's been entertaining watching you run around like a headless chicken."

Loki's jaw tightened. "Who is this? What do you want?"

The voice chuckled darkly. "What I want? I want you to understand how far out of your depth you are. You think you can just play detective and rescue your daughter? You're only making things worse."

"Where is Lila?" Loki demanded, his voice rising.

"Ah, straight to the point. Admirable," the voice replied mockingly. "But I'm not here to give you answers. I'm here to remind you of your place. Watch your step, Mr. Lars. You're treading dangerous ground."

"Listen to me," Loki growled, desperation creeping into his tone. "If you hurt her—"

"Hurt her?" the voice interrupted with a cold laugh. "That depends on you. Keep playing your little games, and you might not like the outcome."

Before Loki could respond, the line went dead.

Loki stared at the phone in his hand, his heart pounding. The taunting tone of the caller's voice echoed in his mind, feeding his frustration and fear.

"What did they say?" Nate asked, his voice tense.

"They're playing games," Loki replied, his hands trembling as he placed the phone on the table. "They didn't give me anything. Just more threats."

Nate stood abruptly, his chair screeching against the floor. "They made a mistake calling you. Every call leaves a trace, no matter how much they try to cover it up."

Loki looked at him, hope flickering in his eyes. "Can you trace it?"

"Maybe," Nate said, already moving toward his laptop. "It's not easy, especially if they used a burner phone or a scrambled line. But I'll do everything I can."

He plugged the phone into his laptop and launched a series of programs. Lines of code filled the screen as Nate's fingers danced over the keyboard, his face illuminated by the soft glow of the monitor.

"It might take some time," Nate muttered, mostly to himself. "They're probably using multiple layers of obfuscation to mask their location."

Minutes dragged by as Loki watched Nate work, the tension in the room palpable. Loki clenched his fists, his mind racing with every possible scenario. What if the caller was right? What if his efforts were only making things worse?

"Anything yet?" Loki asked after what felt like an eternity.

"Almost," Nate replied, not taking his eyes off the screen. "They're good, but not perfect. They left a few digital breadcrumbs. I just need to follow them."

The laptop beeped, and a map appeared on the screen. A red dot blinked on the outskirts of the city, in a remote industrial area surrounded by forests.

Nate's eyes lit up. "I've got it," he said, his voice triumphant. "I've found their location."

Loki's breath caught in his throat as he stared at the screen. The blinking dot felt like a lifeline—a fragile connection to his daughter.

For the first time in days, a glimmer of hope pierced through the darkness.

CHAPTER TWENTY-THREE

The hospital's sterile air and quiet hum were no match for the storm brewing in Loki's mind. After Nate pinpointed the captors' location, it had taken hours of heated discussion between the four of them to agree on the next steps. Loki was still weak, his ribs protesting every movement, but his resolve was ironclad. He refused to sit idle while his daughter's life hung in the balance.

"You're not in any condition to go anywhere," Nate argued, pacing the room.

"I don't care," Loki shot back. "Lila is out there, and I'm not staying behind. Either we all go, or I go alone."

Nate exchanged a hesitant glance with Ian and Max. Finally, he sighed, relenting. "Fine. But you stay in the car. No heroics, okay?"

Loki didn't answer, his silence conveying all they needed to know.

Nate's car, an old 1999 BMW, rumbled along the dark, uneven roads leading to the location. Its once-glossy black paint had dulled over the years, and the occasional squeak from the suspension hinted at its age. It was a car with history—a relic of Nate's father that had seen better days but still had enough life to carry them forward.

"Are you sure about this?" Ian asked from the passenger seat, his voice low.

"No," Loki replied from the back, his eyes fixed on the horizon. "But we don't have a choice."

As they neared the abandoned warehouse, the air grew heavier. The towering structure loomed ahead, its crumbling facade bathed in eerie moonlight. Loki parked the car at a safe distance, its engine idling quietly.

"We'll go in," Nate said, turning to face Loki. "You stay here. Keep the car running, just in case."

Loki nodded reluctantly. "Be careful."

The three of them slipped out of the car and disappeared into the shadows, their figures blending into the dark. Loki watched them go, his heart pounding.

Inside the warehouse, the air was thick with the smell of rust and decay. Nate, Ian, and Max moved cautiously, their footsteps barely audible on the dusty concrete floor. The vast, empty space was filled with rows of abandoned machinery and stacks of wooden crates.

"This place gives me the creeps," Max muttered, glancing around nervously.

"Stay focused," Nate whispered.

They ventured deeper, their eyes scanning for any signs of life. Suddenly, the sound of heavy footsteps echoed through the space. Before they could react, a group of men emerged from the shadows, their faces obscured by masks.

"Look what we have here," one of them sneered, his voice dripping with menace.

The three friends froze, their minds racing.

"Run!" Nate shouted, shoving Ian toward the nearest exit.

They bolted, weaving through the maze of crates and machinery as the gang pursued them. The sound of shouting and pounding footsteps grew louder, closing in with every second.

Outside, Loki sat in the driver's seat, his fingers drumming nervously on the steering wheel. The distant sound of commotion reached his ears, and his stomach sank. He knew something had gone wrong.

Moments later, Nate, Ian, and Max burst out of the warehouse, their faces pale with fear.

"Go! Start driving!" Nate shouted, waving frantically as they sprinted toward the car.

Loki threw the car into gear and began moving, the BMW groaning in protest. The three of them leapt into the backseat just as a group of men poured out of the warehouse, shouting and pointing.

"They've got a car!" Max yelled, looking back.

A black Nissan Navara roared to life, its headlights cutting through the darkness as it sped toward them. Loki pressed harder on the gas, but the old BMW struggled to pick up speed.

"Come on, come on," Loki muttered, his knuckles white as he gripped the wheel.

The Navara closed the gap quickly, its powerful engine growling. The gang inside leaned out of the windows, shouting threats as they gained on the struggling BMW.

"They're going to catch us!" Ian yelled.

"Not if I can help it," Loki growled, his eyes narrowing.

He pushed the car as hard as it would go, swerving onto a narrow dirt path. The BMW's suspension creaked and groaned as it bounced over the uneven terrain, but Loki kept going, his focus unwavering.

The Navara followed closely, its headlights flashing wildly. The gang wasn't giving up easily, and their vehicle's superior power gave them an undeniable advantage.

"Left!" Nate shouted, pointing toward a side road barely visible in the moonlight.

Loki turned sharply, the tires skidding on loose gravel. The BMW fishtailed before regaining traction, but the sudden maneuver gave them a slight lead.

The chase continued, the two vehicles hurtling through the dark countryside. Loki's heart pounded in his chest, every second feeling like an eternity. The old BMW groaned under the strain, but it held together, its legacy as Nate's father's car carrying them forward.

"Keep going!" Nate urged, his voice tinged with desperation.

Loki didn't respond, his focus entirely on the road ahead. He knew they couldn't outrun the Navara forever, but he wasn't about to give up. Not when Lila's life depended on it.

The sound of the Navara's engine roared behind them, a relentless reminder of the danger closing in. But Loki pressed on, determined to stay one step ahead.

83

CHAPTER TWENTY-FOUR

THE REVELATION

The chase had been intense, the air thick with the sound of screeching tires and roaring engines. Loki's heart raced, adrenaline coursing through his veins as the headlights of the pursuing Nissan Navara glared in the rearview mirror. But despite the danger, despite the desperation, his thoughts were focused entirely on one thing—Lila.

They had to find her.

Loki's grip tightened around the steering wheel of Nate's old BMW, the engine rattling beneath him as they made a sharp turn onto a narrow, abandoned street. Nate, Ian, and Max were right behind him, each one of them just as determined, just as desperate to find the clues that would lead them to Lila.

"Pull over here!" Nate urged, his voice sharp and filled with urgency.

Loki slammed on the brakes, the BMW screeching to a halt behind an old, dilapidated building. The tires left black marks on the pavement as he turned off the engine, a heavy silence settling over them all.

They had lost the Navara—for now. Loki let out a shaky breath, his heart still racing from the chase. But he knew they couldn't afford to relax. This was far from over.

"Alright, guys," Loki said, his voice hoarse as he looked at Nate, Ian, and Max. "What did you find?"

Max was the first to answer. "We didn't come back empty-handed." He pulled out a crumpled piece of paper from his jacket pocket, unfolding it with care. Loki's eyes narrowed as he looked at the map, the edges frayed and worn from being carried around.

"I've been going over everything," Nate explained, "and I think we've got something. This place"—he pointed at the map—"this is where they're holding her."

Loki's breath hitched in his chest as he studied the map. His eyes scanned the location that was circled in red. It was a warehouse on the outskirts of the city—isolated, difficult to reach, and perfect for holding someone without being detected.

"This is it," Loki whispered. His heart pounded in his chest. They finally had a lead, a real chance to find Lila.

But just as Loki was about to speak again, his phone buzzed in his pocket. The unknown number had called again. His stomach churned, but this time, he answered the call without hesitation.

"Loki," came the voice on the other end—cold, detached, and menacing. "You've made things a lot harder for yourself."

Loki's jaw clenched. "I don't think you understand. I'm not scared of you. Not anymore."

The voice on the other end chuckled, low and mocking. "You really think you're in control here? You think this is going to end the way you want? You're wrong, Mr. Lars. You're in over your head."

"I don't care what you think," Loki shot back, his voice steady despite the rising tension in his chest. "I know where she is now. And I'm coming for her."

There was a long pause before the voice spoke again. "We're not interested in killing anyone, Loki. But you'll do as we say. The money's what we want. You don't have it, but we'll make sure you get it. You'll get what we want, or there will be consequences."

Loki's eyes narrowed. "What are you really after?"

The voice chuckled again, but this time, it seemed to be tinged with something darker. "You don't get it, do you? We'll tell you whatever you want to hear. But if you don't play along, your daughter's fate will be sealed. This isn't a game, Loki. We're in control."

Before Loki could respond, the line went dead.

"Damn it," Loki muttered under his breath, throwing the phone onto the passenger seat.

"What happened?" Max asked, his voice filled with concern.

Loki's hands gripped the wheel again, his knuckles turning white. "They won't kill her, at least not unless I don't play along. They're not as crazy as I thought. They're playing me. And they'll keep doing it until I give them what they want."

Ian's voice was quiet but firm. "Then we do what we need to do to stop them. We get to her, Loki. We're not backing down."

Loki nodded, his thoughts racing. But before he could say anything more, the sharp pain in his legs flared again, and he winced, clutching his thigh. He hadn't fully recovered from the beating he'd taken, and the long hours of driving had only worsened the ache.

"I can't go any further," Loki said through gritted teeth. His face was pale, and the pain was becoming unbearable. "But you guys—you have to keep going."

Nate stepped forward, concern etched across his face. "What do you mean? We're all in this together, Loki. We'll get you to the warehouse."

Loki shook his head, the pain clouding his vision. "No, I can't do it. You guys go. I'll stay here. I'll rest, but you have to get there. You've already found the location. Just go."

Ian and Max exchanged glances, clearly torn.

"You sure?" Ian asked quietly.

Loki nodded, his jaw clenched tightly. "I'm sure. You've done the hard work. Just get me there, and you'll save her. I'll be right here, waiting for you."

Max looked at him, his expression hardening. "We're not leaving you behind, Loki. But we'll need to take turns. We're getting there together. No one gets left behind."

Loki nodded, grateful for their loyalty. His legs were screaming in pain, but there was no time to rest. "Okay. But someone else needs to drive. My legs... I can't feel them right now."

Nate stepped forward. "I'll drive. You rest, Loki. We're getting her back."

The group quickly loaded into the car, and as they pulled away from the abandoned building, Loki's heart ached with a mixture of hope and fear. He was so close—closer than he had ever been—but the journey wasn't over yet.

They were going to find Lila. No matter what it took.

CHAPTER TWENTY-FIVE

THE PRICE OF A FUTURE

The drive felt longer than it should have, the road ahead stretching out like an endless void, with only the headlights of the car cutting through the darkness. Loki's mind swirled with thoughts—thoughts of Lila, of the kidnappers, and of the past few days that had been nothing short of a nightmare. He rested his head against the window, the pain in his legs a constant reminder of everything he'd been through.

As they drove, Loki's thoughts drifted back to the conversation with the mysterious voice—the one that had promised to release Lila only if he could provide the ransom. But the more he thought about it, the more frustrated he became.

He couldn't just give them the money. He wouldn't.

Ian, who had been driving for the past few miles, broke the silence that had settled between them. "Loki, why don't you just give them the money they want?"

Loki's eyes fluttered open, meeting Ian's gaze. His throat was dry, and he didn't have the energy to explain the complexity of the situation, but Ian's question kept lingering in his mind. "It's not about the money," Loki finally said, his voice hoarse. "It's about the future."

Ian furrowed his brow. "The future?"

Loki's voice grew quieter. "I can't just give them what they want and let them get away with it. If I do, then what's to stop them from doing this to someone else? To someone else's daughter? What if they decide to do this again—take another child, another family? I can't allow that. I won't."

There was a heavy silence in the car, the weight of Loki's words hanging in the air. Max, who had been sitting quietly in the backseat, suddenly spoke up, his voice breaking through the tension.

"Well, Loki, you can always pay them and then go on a shopping spree for yourself. Get yourself a brand-new car, maybe something sporty, you know?"

Loki's lips twitched, but he didn't feel like laughing. Not this time. Max, noticing Loki's lack of reaction, tried again. "I mean, we could all use a little upgrade in our lives, huh? I bet Nate would look good in a convertible. Don't you think, Nate?"

Nate, who was driving, raised an eyebrow, but he didn't respond. Max was always the one to bring humor into dark situations, and though his jokes could be ridiculous at times, they often helped lighten the mood. But not today. Today, Loki was too exhausted, too consumed by the idea of getting Lila back to find any amusement in Max's antics.

But Max wasn't deterred. He leaned forward from the backseat, grinning at Loki. "I mean, if you're paying that ransom, maybe you could ask them for a discount. You know, for being a loyal customer? Just tell them you've been a repeat offender!" He chuckled at his own joke. "Buy one kidnap, get one free. What a deal, huh?"

Loki rolled his eyes, the smallest flicker of a smile almost breaking through. But the truth was, Max's humor wasn't enough to erase the gnawing worry deep inside him. The pain in his legs, the fear for Lila, the question of whether he was doing the right thing—these things were all too much for him to push aside.

"Alright, alright," Loki finally muttered, his voice strained. "Enough of the jokes. I'm not in the mood."

Max raised his hands in mock surrender. "Hey, I get it. Tough crowd tonight."

As the car sped down the deserted road, the distant glow of a few scattered streetlights flickered in the distance. Loki could see the outline of the warehouse on the horizon, the place where Lila was being held. His heart clenched in his chest. He could feel the weight of the moment pressing down on him, the suffocating sense of dread that came with knowing that they were so close to finding her, but still so far away.

Ian broke the silence again, his voice quieter this time. "Loki... do you think she's still okay? You know, after everything that's happened?"

Loki turned his head slightly to look at Ian, his heart heavy with the question. "I don't know. I'm scared, Ian. I don't know what they've done to her. But I can't let them hurt her anymore. I just can't."

Max's voice cut through the tension again, though this time, it was much softer. "We'll get her, Loki. You just have to hang in there. We've got your back."

Loki looked at Max in the rearview mirror, his expression tired but thankful. "I know you do. All of you." He sighed deeply, his hands tightening on the seatbelt. "But what if we're too late? What if they've already..."

He didn't finish the thought. He couldn't. The possibility was too unbearable to even consider.

The car slowed as they neared the location, and Loki could see the outline of the warehouse in the distance. The air felt thicker here, as if the very atmosphere had become laden with tension. They were close now. So close.

Loki's heart raced. His hands gripped the seat, his body tense with anticipation and fear. They were about to enter the lion's den.

"We're here," Nate said quietly, his eyes flicking to the dimly lit warehouse ahead.

Loki nodded. "Alright, let's do this. But stay sharp. No mistakes."

The car came to a stop in the shadows just outside the warehouse. Loki's stomach churned, his breath shallow. This was it. They had made it. But the road ahead was only going to get harder from here.

As the group gathered their things and prepared to move, Loki's mind swirled with questions, doubt, and fear. What if they were too late? What if the kidnappers had already moved Lila? What if, despite everything, they couldn't save her?

But one thing was certain—he wasn't giving up. Not now, not ever.

As the engine was turned off, the night seemed to close in around them, and Loki realized that whatever happened next, there would be no turning back.

CHAPTER TWENTY-SIX

THE BLOODIED TABLE

Loki's heart hammered in his chest as he limped toward the entrance of the warehouse. Ian had taken the lead, but Loki's legs were too weak from the beating he had taken earlier. He leaned heavily on Ian's shoulder, the weight of his body dragging him down as they stumbled through the shadows. Despite the dull pain in his legs, his mind was sharper than ever, focused solely on the one thing that mattered most—finding Lila.

Max and Nate followed behind them, their footsteps muffled on the concrete floor as they entered the building. The warehouse was dark, save for a few flickering lights overhead. The air was thick, laden with the scent of rust and something metallic—a smell that immediately sent a chill down Loki's spine.

"Stay alert," Loki whispered, his voice strained as they slowly moved deeper into the warehouse. Every step felt like an eternity, the tension in the air palpable. Loki could feel the weight of his breath, the quickening of his pulse as he peered into the darkness ahead. The warehouse was eerily quiet, but something about it felt wrong.

As they rounded a corner, Loki's eyes caught something—something that made his stomach churn. There, in the corner of the room, were various weapons laid out on a table: axes, knives, and other brutal tools, each one stained with blood. The sight of the blood sent a jolt through Loki, a cold wave washing over him. He had seen violence before, but never like this. This wasn't just some random crime—it was organized. Planned. Methodical.

"Stay close," Loki muttered to Ian, trying to steady himself despite the ache in his legs.

As they continued to move forward, their eyes scanned the room, looking for any sign of Lila. And then, through the dim light, Loki saw her.

Lila was tied to a chair in the center of the room, her head hanging limp and her body unmoving. Her face was pale, her eyes closed, and there was a strip of cello tape across her mouth. A wave of panic surged through Loki, his breath catching in his throat. His heart felt like it was about to burst out of his chest.

"Ian, that's her," Loki gasped, his voice hoarse with emotion.

Ian immediately nodded, a mix of relief and concern in his eyes. "Loki, we've got her. We've got to get her out of here."

Ignoring the pain in his legs, Loki pushed forward. Every step felt like it took all his energy, but he didn't care. His daughter was there, so close. He reached out, grabbing Ian's shoulder for support as they made their way to her. Loki's eyes were locked on her, desperate, terrified. His daughter—his sweet, brave daughter—was alive. But how long would she remain so?

When they reached her, Loki's hands trembled as he gently brushed her hair away from her face. "Lila," he whispered, his voice cracking. "Lila, wake up. It's me, Dad."

He reached for the cello tape, trying to peel it away from her mouth. He could feel his pulse racing, his breath shallow, the urgency of the moment making everything feel hazy. Lila's face was bruised, her clothes torn, but she was still breathing. That was all that mattered. She was still alive.

But before Loki could pull the tape off, something hard and cold collided with the back of Ian's head. The sound of metal meeting bone echoed through the room, and Ian staggered forward, his eyes wide with shock. He hadn't seen the blow coming.

Loki's heart skipped a beat as he turned to see who had attacked them.

A massive figure stood in the shadows—tall, broad-shouldered, and covered in muscle. He was holding a metal rod, the end of which was slick with blood. The man's eyes glinted with malice, and a sadistic smile spread across his face as he watched Ian fall to the ground.

"Ian!" Loki shouted, his voice full of panic. He lunged forward, but the man was already moving toward him.

The large man swung the metal rod again, this time aiming directly for Loki. He barely managed to dodge the blow, his legs barely able to keep him steady. Sweat poured down his face as he stumbled backward, his eyes wide with fear and confusion.

Max and Nate rushed to Ian's side, trying to help him, but the man was already advancing, his eyes cold and calculating.

"You shouldn't have come here, Loki," the man said, his voice low and menacing. "You should've just stayed out of it. But now... now you've made it personal."

Loki's heart pounded in his chest as he watched the man step closer, his grip tightening on the metal rod. "What do you want with my daughter?" Loki demanded, trying to steady his breathing despite the terror coursing through him.

The man didn't answer. He just swung the rod again, this time aiming for Loki's head. But Loki ducked, narrowly avoiding the blow, and for the first time, he felt the full weight of the danger surrounding him.

In that moment, he knew they were out of their depth. They were in a fight they couldn't win, and things were about to get much worse.

But there was no way in hell Loki was going to let them take his daughter again. He would fight to his last breath if he had to.

But before he could make a move, the sound of approaching footsteps echoed from the hallway, and Loki's stomach dropped.

The man stopped, his head snapping toward the noise. The tension in the room was thick, and Loki's pulse was pounding in his ears. This wasn't over. Not by a long shot.

95

CHAPTER TWENTY-SEVEN

THE FIGHT FOR FREEDOM

Loki's heart raced in his chest as he heard the crunching of gravel outside the warehouse. The big man in front of him was only a few feet away, his eyes gleaming with malice. Loki's fingers shook as he tried to peel the cello tape off Lila's mouth, but his hands weren't steady enough. His mind was consumed by panic and fear for his daughter, but deep inside, something sparked—a flicker of defiance.

"I'll get you out of here, Lila. I promise," Loki whispered, his voice hoarse. His eyes filled with tears, but he wiped them away, not wanting her to see how broken he was. His daughter—his precious little girl—was still breathing. Still alive. That was all that mattered.

Suddenly, the silence was shattered by a loud thwack. Loki turned, seeing the massive man swing the metal rod toward him again. He ducked, his heart racing as the rod narrowly missed his head. He scrambled to get closer to Lila, but before he could make it, the man's thick hand shot out and grabbed his shoulder, forcing him back.

Max and Nate were already on their feet, trying to help Ian, who had collapsed from the blow to the back of his head. But they weren't going to let that stop them. Nate, his eyes steely with determination, lunged at the man with the rod, while Max grabbed a nearby piece of broken wood. The two friends weren't about to let

Loki face this alone.

"Get out of the way, Loki!" Nate shouted, dodging another swing from the rod-wielding man.

Loki nodded, his breath heavy, but his focus was still on Lila. He could hear the sounds of the fight erupting behind him, the clash of metal against wood, the grunts and shouts, but none of it mattered. The only thing that mattered was getting Lila out of there.

With trembling fingers, Loki managed to tear the tape from her mouth, but her head hung limply to the side. He shook her gently.

"Lila... Lila, wake up, baby," he pleaded.

Lila's eyelids fluttered, but she didn't wake up completely. Loki's heart sank. She was barely conscious. His worst fear had been that they would hurt her too much. But she was alive—alive, and that was the sliver of hope that kept him going.

Suddenly, Loki heard the unmistakable sound of footsteps coming from deeper within the warehouse. The faintest sound at first, but then it grew louder, heavier. A wave of dread washed over him. The gang had arrived.

His blood ran cold. They weren't alone anymore.

The door at the far end of the room slammed open, and several men in dark clothes poured into the room. There were at least six of them. Their eyes were cold, and their faces were hardened by a life of violence. Loki counted them quickly—six men, including the one with the metal rod.

One of the men—a tall, lanky figure with a scar running down his face—stepped forward and smirked at Loki. "So, you think you can just come in here and take your daughter?" he sneered. "It doesn't work that way, buddy."

Loki didn't say anything. His fists clenched at his sides. He wasn't going to beg. He wasn't going to plead. He was going to fight for his daughter, no matter what it took.

Max and Nate, still locked in combat with the big guy, exchanged a glance. Nate was already breathing heavily, sweat dripping down his face, but he wasn't backing down. He swung a quick punch at the big man's gut, but the man grinned and caught Nate's fist in midair.

With a swift motion, the man shoved Nate to the side. But before he could react, Max took a solid swing at the man's jaw, knocking him back a few steps.

Loki turned his attention back to Lila. His hands were shaking as he carefully untied the rope that bound her to the chair. He had to be quick, but the knots were too tight, the rope too thick. His fingers trembled with fear and desperation.

"Lila... Lila, I need you to wake up," he whispered urgently, his voice breaking. He pulled harder at the ropes, his frustration mounting.

That's when a loud bang rang through the room, followed by a sharp crack.

Loki's head snapped to the side, just in time to see the lanky man draw a gun from his waistband. The men had come prepared. Loki's blood ran cold as he realized the stakes had just been raised. The gun was aimed directly at him.

But then something happened.

In a blur of motion, Max lunged forward, tackling the man with the gun to the ground. The gun slipped from the man's grip, skidding across the floor. The two struggled, rolling across the concrete, each trying to overpower the other. Loki's breath caught in his throat as he saw the gun on the ground just inches away from them. It was now or never.

Without thinking, Loki quickly grabbed the gun, his fingers closing around the cold metal. He didn't hesitate. He had no choice but to act. He pointed the gun at the closest thug—one of the men who had been standing by, watching the chaos unfold. The thug froze, his face registering shock and fear.

"Move and I'll shoot," Loki growled, his voice rough but determined.

The thug held his hands up in surrender, backing away slowly, his eyes never leaving the gun. Loki's heart was pounding in his chest, but his focus remained sharp. He had the gun now. He had the upper hand.

But then, as if on cue, more footsteps echoed through the warehouse. More men were coming. Loki could hear their heavy boots pounding against the floor, the unmistakable sound of reinforcements.

Loki's grip tightened on the gun. This was far from over.

With a sudden movement, one of the thugs behind him lunged toward him, but Max, still struggling with the lanky man, saw the threat and threw a fist into the thug's face. Nate, not far behind, grabbed a nearby metal pipe and swung it at another approaching thug, knocking him to the ground.

Loki didn't waste a second. He grabbed Lila's unconscious body, lifting her with the help of Ian, who had regained consciousness. He cradled her to his chest, his eyes scanning the room frantically as he tried to plan their escape.

Then he heard the sound of more footsteps. The entire gang was closing in. And in that moment, Loki realized—this fight was far from over. The odds were against them. But Loki had already come too far. He wasn't going to let anything happen to his daughter.

"No one is taking her from me again," Loki muttered under his breath, his voice fierce with determination.

And with that, the fight for freedom began.

THE SHADOW IN THE CLOAK

The air in the warehouse was thick with smoke and the acrid scent of fear. Loki's breath came in ragged gasps, his chest heaving from exertion. He still held the gun firmly in his grip, eyes scanning the room for any movement. The fight had been chaotic—he wasn't sure how many men he'd shot, how many were still alive, but one thing was for sure: it had been brutal.

The remaining gang members were retreating, backing up against the far wall, clearly rattled by Loki's sudden, wild onslaught. His hands shook, not from fear, but from adrenaline and exhaustion. He had only one goal in mind: getting Lila to safety. She was still unconscious, her head leaning against his shoulder as he cradled her in his arms. Her body felt so small in his grip, and every time he looked down at her pale face, a wave of guilt washed over him.

"Loki, move!" Max shouted, struggling to stay on his feet as he swung a pipe at one of the thugs who had been about to charge them. His face was smeared with dirt and sweat, but his eyes were fierce with determination. Nate, too, was still holding his own, fighting back with everything he had. They weren't giving up.

The gunfire had stopped for now, but Loki wasn't about to lower his weapon. The danger wasn't over—he could feel it. The warehouse was filled with tense silence as they waited for the next attack, every corner shadowed, every sound magnified.

Suddenly, the sound of heavy footsteps broke through the tense silence. It wasn't one of the gang members rushing to attack, nor was it a stray thug trying to sneak up on them. No—these footsteps were slow, deliberate, each one echoing in the stillness like a signal of doom.

Loki stiffened, his grip on the gun tightening, his eyes searching the shadows. Whoever it was, they weren't hiding. They weren't trying to sneak up on him. This person had no fear.

And then, from the dark doorway, he saw him. The figure stepped slowly into the dim light, moving with the kind of calm precision that sent a chill straight down Loki's spine.

He was old—older than Loki had imagined anyone could be in this line of work. His face was lined with deep wrinkles, his eyes shadowed beneath heavy brows, and his expression... cold. The man moved deliberately, almost as if he were savoring the moment, enjoying the chaos, the suffering.

But it wasn't his age or appearance that made Loki's stomach tighten—it was the eerie familiarity. There was something about him, something that gnawed at the edges of Loki's memory, but he couldn't quite place it.

The man was dressed in a long black cloak that billowed slightly as he moved, his feet making no sound against the cracked concrete floor. His clothes were dark—black slacks, a black shirt beneath the cloak—and he looked like someone who didn't belong in the world Loki knew. He looked out of place, as though he had stepped out of some nightmare or dark tale.

Loki's breath caught in his throat. There was a stillness in the air as the old man stopped just inside the room, standing tall, his eyes fixed directly on Loki.

Loki could feel his heart pounding in his chest, his mind scrambling for any trace of recognition. Who was this man? Why did he look so familiar? Had he seen him before? Was this some sort of twisted trick?

The old man's gaze was chilling, devoid of emotion, yet there was an air of authority about him, a silent power that made Loki's skin crawl. He didn't speak at first, just stared at Loki, his dark eyes studying him like a predator appraising its prey.

"Loki..." the old man's voice was low, cold, and it sent a shiver down Loki's spine. "You've come so far. But you should know... there are consequences for crossing us."

The words echoed in the warehouse, making every inch of the room feel colder. The gun in Loki's hand felt heavier suddenly, like it was no longer enough. He tightened his grip, but there was a growing sense of dread gnawing at him. This man was no ordinary thug. This was someone much more dangerous.

The old man's lips curled into a faint smile, but it didn't reach his eyes. He took a step forward, his movements slow, deliberate. "You think you can just walk into our world and take what you want, Loki? Your daughter... is nothing more than a pawn in a much larger game. You've made a grave mistake."

Loki's pulse quickened. He wasn't sure who this man was or how he was connected to everything, but he knew one thing for certain: this was the one who was truly pulling the strings. And he was about to find out just how deep this nightmare went.

The silence stretched between them, thick with tension. Loki's thoughts raced, his mind scrambling to make sense of the situation. But no matter how hard he tried, he couldn't find any answers.

He had no idea who this man was. But he knew that the true fight was just beginning.

As the man took another step forward, Loki tensed, ready for anything. The old man's voice cut through the air again, smooth and chilling.

"Did you really think you could save her, Loki?"

Loki's heart hammered. He was in no position to fight back—his body was tired, his legs were shaking, and his gun was barely in his grasp. But he wouldn't give in. Not now. Not when Lila needed him most.

The man's cold eyes bore into Loki's, and he smiled again—a smile that promised nothing but pain.

Loki took a step back, raising the gun, his finger hovering over the trigger.

But the old man just laughed softly, his voice devoid of any warmth. "You're too late, Loki."

CHAPTER TWENTY-NINE

THE TRUTH

The warehouse was eerily silent, save for the soft echo of the old man's steps as he moved closer to Loki. The room, once filled with the sounds of gunshots and screams, had fallen into an unsettling calm. Loki's breath was shallow, his chest tight with fear and uncertainty. His grip on the gun was faltering as his mind raced, trying to make sense of everything that had happened.

The man in the black cloak—he knew something Loki didn't. There was an unmistakable presence about him, a familiarity that gnawed at Loki's every thought. His mind searched through the fog of confusion, trying to place the pieces together. He had seen this man before. But where?

Then, suddenly, it clicked. The realization hit him like a freight train, and his blood ran cold.

"No..." Loki whispered under his breath, the word barely escaping his lips.

His mind flashed back—years ago, a shadow in the background of his past. The details were hazy, but he could see the man's face now, clearly, in his memories. This was the man who had been lurking behind it all.

"Marcus..." Loki shouted, his voice filled with shock and disbelief. "It's you!"

The old man's lips curved into a small, cruel smile as he took another slow step forward, his eyes never leaving Loki's face. The air felt thick with tension, and Loki's heart pounded in his chest.

"Ah, so you remember me," Marcus replied in a calm, almost amused tone. "I must say, I'm impressed. You've done well to make it this far."

Loki's mind was spinning. He had known Marcus before, years ago, during a time when things had been much simpler. But Marcus had disappeared from his life—vanished without a trace. And now, here he was, standing in front of him, with Lila's life hanging in the balance.

"What... what do you want from me?" Loki demanded, his voice trembling with a mix of fear and anger.

Marcus chuckled softly, shaking his head. "You still don't understand, do you? You think this is about money, or power, or vengeance. It's not. It's about control."

Loki's grip on his gun tightened, his knuckles white. "Why Lila? Why my daughter?"

Marcus' smile grew wider, his cold eyes gleaming with something dark and malicious. "Because she's the perfect bait, Loki. You've been so busy trying to be the hero, trying to fix everything. But the truth is, you never saw the real game we were playing. Your daughter? She's the key to making sure you'll never escape."

Loki's heart raced as the pieces of the puzzle began to come together. This wasn't just about money or revenge—it was about something far more sinister. Lila's kidnapping wasn't a random act. It was carefully planned, orchestrated by someone who knew exactly how to pull his strings.

But before Loki could say anything else, the man's demeanor shifted. The smile faded from Marcus' face as he reached into his coat pocket and pulled out a sleek, black handgun. Loki's breath caught in his throat as the man aimed it directly at him.

Loki's body tensed. His mind screamed for him to act, but before he could even lift his gun, Marcus spoke.

"You're too late, Loki," Marcus said coldly, his voice filled with finality. "You've lost."

And in an instant, the gunshot rang out.

Loki's eyes widened as the sound of the bullet firing echoed in the small room. Time seemed to slow as he saw the bullet leave the barrel of the gun, headed straight for him. The world around him blurred. He couldn't move fast enough. He was too weak, too exhausted, to dodge.

But just as the bullet was about to reach him, a force slammed into his side, knocking him off balance.

Everything happened in a blur.

Loki hit the ground hard, the breath knocked out of him as he landed on his back. For a brief, terrifying moment, he thought he had been shot. But when he looked up, he saw Ian, his face pale, his eyes wide with shock.

"Ian!" Loki shouted, his voice cracking with horror.

Ian collapsed beside him, a pained groan escaping his lips. Blood oozed from the side of his chest, staining his shirt. He had taken the bullet for Loki, sacrificing himself without a second thought.

"No... no, Ian!" Loki gasped, panic rising in his chest. "Why... why would you do that?!"

Ian's lips curled into a weak smile as he looked at Loki, his breath coming in shallow gasps. "I... I couldn't let you die, Loki. Not like this. You... you've been through enough."

Loki's eyes blurred with tears as he held Ian, trying desperately to stem the bleeding. His hands shook, his heart pounding in his chest as he tried to make sense of what was happening. Ian had saved his life, but now it was too late—there was no time. The gunshot had done its damage, and Ian was slipping away.

The world seemed to stop around Loki, and all he could focus on was Ian's fading breath. The pain was unbearable, and it was only made worse by the haunting reality of what had just happened.

As Loki held Ian in his arms, he heard Marcus' voice, cold and distant in the background.

"You've failed, Loki. And now, your friend will pay the price."

Loki's eyes snapped toward Marcus, his anger rising like a tide. He wanted to scream, to rage against everything that had brought them to this point. But Ian was slipping away, and he couldn't afford to lose another person he loved.

Loki glanced down at Ian, his voice filled with desperation.

"Don't you die on me, Ian... please."

But Ian's eyes were already starting to close. His breathing slowed, and Loki's heart shattered as he realized that there was nothing more he could do.

And just like that, the world around him went black.

CHAPTER THIRTY

Loki's hands were trembling, his chest rising and falling with each breath. The weight of Ian's sacrifice was suffocating him, threatening to drown him in waves of guilt and grief. As he watched Ian's lifeless body on the ground, a fire ignited within him—fury that had been building up for so long finally bursting to the surface.

Without thinking, he rose to his feet, his body still aching from the earlier blows he had suffered. But none of that mattered now. The only thing that mattered was avenging Ian, ending this nightmare, and stopping Marcus. The man who had orchestrated all of this. The man who had taken everything from him.

Loki's eyes locked onto Marcus, who stood cold and composed, watching him with a detached, almost amused expression. The man was so calm, so sure of himself, but Loki could feel his rage building, a wild storm that refused to be contained.

In one swift motion, Loki lunged at Marcus, catching him off guard. The old man was knocked backward, stumbling to the ground as Loki pinned him beneath him, his hands gripping Marcus by the collar. Loki's heart was pounding, his blood boiling. Every punch he threw felt like a release, a desperate attempt to rid himself of the pain.

Fist after fist, Loki struck Marcus in the face, each blow harder than the last. The sound of bone meeting flesh echoed in the room, and with each punch, Loki's anger intensified. His vision blurred with fury, the world around him dissolving into a haze of red.

"Why?!" Loki shouted, his voice raw with emotion. "Why did you do this?!"

Marcus didn't answer. His lips curled into a small, mocking smile as blood trickled from his nose. The old man's eyes glinted with a cold, calculating look, as if he were enjoying every moment of Loki's torment. But Loki didn't care. The rage was consuming him, and he kept punching, his fists becoming a blur of motion.

He punched Marcus again, and this time, blood sprayed from the man's nose, splattering across Loki's face. But still, Marcus didn't beg for mercy. Still, he didn't show any sign of fear.

Loki's heart pounded in his chest as he pulled back, his breath coming in ragged gasps. He was exhausted, his body aching from the strain, but he wasn't done. Not yet.

With a final surge of strength, Loki drew back his fist and slammed it into Marcus' face one last time. This time, the old man's head snapped back with a sickening crack, and he fell limp beneath Loki's weight.

For a moment, there was only silence. Loki's hands were covered in blood, his knuckles raw and swollen from the relentless assault. His chest heaved with each breath, the adrenaline coursing through his veins, but even in the midst of his anger, something inside him felt... hollow.

Marcus was still alive, barely. His bloodied face was unrecognizable, his breathing shallow and labored. Loki, his face twisted in anguish, knew what he had to do.

Reaching for the gun that had been dropped earlier, Loki picked it up with trembling hands. The cold metal felt foreign in his grip, like it wasn't even a part of him. But he couldn't stop now. He had come this far, and there was no turning back. Not after everything that had happened.

With a look of pure hatred, Loki aimed the gun at Marcus' forehead. His mind screamed in protest, but his heart—his broken, shattered heart—overruled it. He squeezed the trigger.

The shot rang out, deafening in the silence.

Marcus' body jerked violently as the bullet hit its mark, the force of the impact sending him sprawling back onto the cold floor. His lifeless eyes stared up at the ceiling, his expression frozen in a mask of shock and pain.

Loki stood over him, his chest heaving, the weight of what he had just done crashing down on him. His hands were still shaking, the blood on them feeling like it was never going to come off. He had just taken a life—taken Marcus' life. And for what? Revenge? Justice? To protect his daughter?

But it didn't feel like justice. It didn't feel like protection. It felt like a terrible mistake.

Loki staggered back, dropping the gun as his legs gave out beneath him. He collapsed to the ground, his back against the wall, his eyes fixed on Marcus' lifeless form. Tears welled up in his eyes, but he didn't move to wipe them away. He let them fall, letting his grief take over.

He had just killed someone. Someone who had been behind the pain and suffering of his family. But even as he felt a sense of finality, he felt no relief. No closure. Just emptiness.

Loki's heart ached for Ian, for everything he had lost. The man who had been his closest friend, the one who had stood by him through everything, was now gone. The weight of the loss crushed him. He couldn't save Ian. He couldn't save anyone.

He had failed.

His tears fell faster now, the pain too much to bear. His sobs wracked his body, and for the first time in a long time, Loki felt utterly broken. He had done everything in his power to save his family, but it hadn't been enough.

He had become the thing he hated most.

Loki buried his face in his hands, overwhelmed by the sorrow and guilt that consumed him. His best friend was dead. His daughter was still in danger. And he had just killed a man. He didn't know how to live with that.

The sound of footsteps echoed in the distance, but Loki didn't move. He couldn't. All he could do was sit there, lost in his grief, wondering how he had let everything spiral so far out of control.

And as the world continued to spin around him, Loki realized that the fight wasn't over. But at that moment, he wasn't sure he had the strength to keep going.

Max and Nate were kneeling beside Ian, their faces pale, but there was no energy left to speak. They had lost their friend, their comrade—their family.

Loki could barely hear them, couldn't comprehend what was happening around him. His heart was still heavy, the weight of Ian's death unbearable. There was no light at the end of this tunnel, no happy ending, no redemption.

The room felt cold, distant. The faces around him were a blur. The only thing that remained clear in his mind was the image of Ian's lifeless body.

And in that silence, Loki cried. He cried for his best friend. He cried for his daughter. And he cried for the man he had just become.

CHAPTER THIRTY-ONE

The morning sky was overcast, the sun hidden behind thick, grey clouds that seemed to mourn alongside those gathered. Loki stood at the edge of the small cemetery, his face etched with exhaustion, pain, and the weight of everything that had transpired. His left leg was still weak, supported by a crutch, but the physical pain was nothing compared to the ache in his heart.

The burial ground was eerily quiet except for the sound of rustling leaves in the cold breeze. Ian's coffin, a simple oak box adorned with a bouquet of white lilies, rested at the centre of the crowd. His mother, an elderly woman with kind but broken eyes, sat in the front row, her wrinkled hands trembling as she clutched a handkerchief. Nate and Max stood nearby, their faces pale, trying to remain stoic but failing as tears slipped silently down their cheeks.

Loki swallowed hard, his throat dry. He didn't know how he had made it here. He didn't feel worthy of standing amongst Ian's loved ones, let alone being the one they looked to for answers. He had promised to protect Ian, and now... Ian was gone. A hero. A friend. A brother.

Lila stood beside him, her small frame wrapped in an oversized black coat. She looked so fragile, her face pale and her eyes puffy from crying. Her hands clutched at Loki's arm, as if afraid to let go, afraid that he too might disappear. But the guilt on her face was unmistakable, and it tore Loki apart.

"Daddy..." she whispered, her voice trembling.

He glanced down at her, his heart breaking at the sight of her tear-streaked face. He knew she blamed herself. She hadn't said it outright, but the way she avoided his gaze, the way she flinched whenever Ian's name was mentioned, made it clear.

"It's not your fault, Lila," Loki said softly, his voice barely audible. He crouched down, ignoring the pain shooting through his legs, and gently cupped her face. "Do you hear me? None of this is your fault."

Her lips quivered, and she shook her head. "But... if I hadn't gone out that day... if I'd just stayed home..."

"Lila," Loki interrupted, his tone firm yet filled with love. "Stop. You didn't do anything wrong. You went out because you wanted to live your life, to be a kid, to enjoy your friends. What happened wasn't your fault. The blame lies with the monsters who chose to hurt us, not you."

She broke into sobs, and Loki pulled her into his arms, holding her tightly. His own tears fell silently as he stroked her hair, whispering words of comfort even as his own heart shattered into pieces.

The service began, and the priest's voice echoed solemnly through the cemetery. Loki didn't hear most of it; his mind was a storm of memories. Ian laughing at one of Max's terrible jokes. Ian stays up all night with him to plan their next move. Ian took that bullet, saving his life without a second thought.

When it was time to lower the coffin, Loki found himself walking forward, each step feeling like a thousand pounds. He placed his hand on the polished wood, his fingers trembling.

"I'm sorry, Ian," he whispered, his voice cracking. "I'm so, so sorry."

Nate placed a comforting hand on Loki's shoulder, his own face a mask of grief. "He wouldn't want you to blame yourself," Nate said softly. "He did what he did because he cared. For you. For Lila. For all of us."

Loki nodded, but the weight in his chest didn't lessen. As the coffin was lowered into the ground, Lila clutched his hand tightly, her small fingers digging into his palm. Together, they watched as the man who had sacrificed everything for them was laid to rest.

The next morning, Loki found himself sitting in a cold, sterile courtroom. The verdict was as expected: five years for manslaughter, reduced from ten due to self-defence. But it didn't feel like justice to Loki. Nothing about this felt just.

As the guards prepared to escort him out, Loki was given a few moments with his daughter. They were alone in a small, grey room, the air heavy with unspoken words. Lila stood in front of him, her head bowed, her hands clenched into fists.

"Daddy..." she began, but her voice cracked, and she couldn't continue.

Loki knelt, wincing as his injured leg protested, and placed his hands on her shoulders. "Lila, look at me."

She hesitated before lifting her tear-filled eyes to meet his. "I'm so sorry," she choked out. "This is all my fault. If I hadn't gone out that day..."

"Lila," Loki interrupted, his voice firm but gentle. "I told you before, and I'll tell you again. This is not your fault. You are my daughter, my everything, and I would do it all over again if it meant keeping you safe."

She threw herself into his arms, clutching him tightly as sobs wracked her small body. Loki held her close, burying his face in her hair, his own tears streaming freely.

"I'm going to miss you so much," she whispered. "Five years is too long."

Loki pulled back just enough to look at her, his hands gently cupping her face. "Five years will go by faster than you think. And when I get out, we'll start over. A new life. Just you and me."

She nodded, but her tears didn't stop. "Promise me you'll be okay."

"I promise," Loki said, though he wasn't sure if it was a promise he could keep.

He kissed her forehead, his lips lingering as if trying to memorize the feeling. Then he stood, his movements slow and painful, and allowed the guards to lead him away. He didn't look back. He couldn't. If he did, he knew he wouldn't be able to leave.

As the prison gates closed behind him, Loki felt the full weight of his new reality. The next five years would be long, gruelling, and lonely. But for Lila, for Ian, for everyone who had sacrificed for him, he would endure.

In the distance, he imagined Ian's voice, laughing at some inside joke they had shared. And for a moment, a small, bittersweet smile tugged at Loki's lips.

He would carry their memories with him, no matter how heavy they were. And one day, he would find peace.

Q & A Section

Let's see how careful you have been reading...

1. What do you think motivated Loki to keep going despite the overwhelming challenges he faced?

2. How did the relationship between Loki and Lila evolve throughout the story?

3. Were there moments in the story that made you reflect on your relationships or experiences?

4. What themes stood out to you the most in this story?

5. How did the ending resonate with you? Would you have made different choices if you were in Loki's shoes?

About The Author

R.K. DARSHAAN is a passionate storyteller who loves creating narratives that captivate and inspire. With a lifelong love for writing, they weave tales that explore deep emotions, thrilling adventures, and the resilience of the human spirit. When not writing, Darshaan enjoys spending time in nature, reading, and finding inspiration in the everyday moments of life. Their dedication to crafting memorable stories continues to drive their work, resonating with readers from all walks of life.

www.ingramcontent.com/pod-product-compliance
Lightning Source LLC
Chambersburg PA
CBHW031148130726
47988CB00006B/2593